'Get a grip, Anni,' I mutter under my breath. 'Come on, how can anyone have broken in?'

I stand at the top of the main staircase, not daring to switch on the landing light again. If there's an intruder here, he won't be able to see me. And I, at least, can find my way around the house in the dark.

I turn right. Two of the rooms on this side are always kept locked because of broken floorboards. But my old bedroom is here, also the master bedroom, a bathroom and my dad's study. I'm going to search these four now, before I lose my nerve. I have to steel myself to take hold of the handle and open the first door.

My room is ghostly, silent and filthy with dust, a large space in the middle where the bed used to be, the walls pinned with torn photos of fluffy kittens, cute dogs and boy bands that split up months ago. It's like somewhere I lived in a former life.

I boldly turn on the light, but my heart is jumping with fear, my pulse skittering. There's nowhere for anyone to hide except the wardrobe. Without thinking what I'll do if someone jumps out at me, I wrench the mirrored doors apart.

13
HOURS

NARINDER DHAMI

Tamarind

THIRTEEN HOURS
A TAMARIND BOOK 978 1 848 53116 1

First published in Great Britain by Tamarind Books,
an imprint of Random House Children's Publishers UK
A Penguin Random House Company

Penguin
Random House
UK

This edition published 2015

1 3 5 7 9 10 8 6 4 2

Text copyright © Narinder Dhami, 2015

Penguin Random House is committed to a sustainable future for
our business, our readers and our planet. This book is made from
Forest Stewardship Council® certified paper.

MIX
Paper from
responsible sources
FSC® C016897

Set in 11/20 pt Sabon by Falcon Oast Graphic Art Ltd.

Tamarind Books are published by Random House Children's Publishers UK,
61–63 Uxbridge Road, London W5 5SA

www.tamarindbooks.co.uk
www.randomhousechildrens.co.uk
www.randomhouse.co.uk

Addresses for companies within The Random House Group Limited
can be found at: www.randomhouse.co.uk/offices.htm

THE RANDOM HOUSE GROUP Limited Reg. No. 954009

A CIP catalogue record for this book is available from the British Library.

Printed and bound in Great Britain by CPI Group (UK) Ltd, Croydon CR0 4YY

Friday 7 November, 3.42 p.m.

My life runs like clockwork. Nothing can go wrong, ever, because it could mean the difference between life or death. And I'm not joking.

When the school bell signals freedom at 3.45 p.m. exactly, I always make a break for it. I run and I run, never stopping. Our house is 1.8 miles away, and I *must* be home by five minutes past four. No ifs or buts. There's no other way to make it on time except to run the whole way. Whatever it takes, I can't be late. *I will not be late.*

It doesn't matter where my last lesson of the day takes place. Wherever I am, I know the quickest way out of the school building. I learned the location of every classroom, staircase and exit the first day I arrived at Hayesford Secondary School in September, just two months ago.

Last lesson this Friday afternoon is a double dose of French. Hiding away in a corner, still and silent, merging into the background, I keep my head down so the teacher doesn't notice me. It's what I'm good at. As usual, I watch the minutes tick away on the clock, and I count them down.

I have a routine, and today is no different. Three minutes before the bell, I slip books, pens and papers into my bag underneath the table. My jacket is already rolled up and bundled inside, placed there at lunch time. I grasp the handles of my bag tightly. No one notices.

Come on, I think, clockwatching obsessively, counting down inside my head. Come *on*. The sixty seconds between 3.44 and 3.45 p.m. seem like six hundred, always.

Then the bell rings and I snap my laptop shut, although I leave it on the desk because it's not mine; it belongs to the school – I can't afford my own. I slide from my chair, and before my classmates have even begun to pack away their stuff, I'm through the door.

Behind me Mrs Kaye is still talking. 'Have a good weekend, everyone, and don't forget, I want your homework in by—'

But I'm gone, expertly pulling my jacket from my bag and slipping it on as I speed down the corridor. Homework is the very least of my problems.

Quite often I'm first into the playground with a clear run to the open gates. But if my last lesson of the day is at the other end of the school, as it is today, there will already be students outside before I get there, and they keep coming, flowing endlessly out of the building from every exit. They hang around in groups, chatting, laughing, texting, snapping selfies, standing in my way, slowing me down as I swerve round them.

Today one of the big boys tries to trip me up as I fly past, for a laugh. But I'm ready for him, hurdling his outstretched leg, and then I'm out of the playground into the street. After a mild, golden autumn, winter is creeping in, curling her freezing fingers around us, and already the light is fading into dusk. But my heart lifts because today is Friday and I'm free of school for two whole days. Once I get home, though, I won't leave the house except to buy food and – well, you don't need to know the details.

The school buses wait at the gate. One of them

stops near my home and would get me there in just ten minutes. But I don't have the money for the bus. I never do.

I run to a strict schedule. It should take four minutes to reach the shops a few streets away, so when I get to Tesco Express, I glance at my watch. Four minutes exactly.

I'm flying along so fast that my inky-black hair, which has never been cut and reaches below my waist when it's loose, is slipping from its ponytail. I neatly sidestep the bustling shoppers, wondering briefly what they think of me. I know what they see – a small, slight figure with dark eyes, too big in a thin face, and a permanently anxious expression.

I dodge round the long queue for the cash machine outside the bank.

'Look where you're going!' a woman in a smart coat snaps at me. I was never anywhere near her, but she has a narrow, mean mouth and probably speaks like that to everyone she meets. At times I long for a big family and lots of friends. Then someone like the mean woman comes along, and I'm glad it's just me and Mum.

To the post office on the corner – five minutes. I'm still on schedule.

Then anxiety grips and twists my insides as I see that the pavement outside the post office has been dug up by workmen. The area is cordoned off and a sign directs people to a narrow, single-file walkway. I stop to assess the situation in a split-second. Is it quicker to cross the busy road and so avoid the hole in the pavement altogether? Or will the time spent waiting for the traffic lights to change so that I can cross the road make me even later?

Panting, gulping in lungfuls of air, I decide to stay where I am, and I join the queue of people waiting to pass along the walkway. Others are coming from the opposite direction and we have to wait because there isn't room for two lines of people, and they keep coming and we keep waiting.

Hurry! Hurry! Hurry! I scream silently, the words pulsing inside my head. Terrifying images of what might be happening at home if I don't make it there on time flash through my mind, rewinding and replaying over and over again, ruthless, relentless.

Now panic sets in. I glance at my watch every couple of seconds, shifting from one foot to the other, praying for a break in the endless stream of people.

I should have crossed the road, I think, angry with myself, with the workmen who dug up the pavement and with the people who don't let me pass. I should have crossed the road!

A mother with a baby in a buggy is the last person to negotiate her way carefully along the walkway towards us. The buggy is wide and the walkway is narrow and it seems to take her hours to reach the other end where we're all waiting, while the baby sits upright in his seat like a cute, chubby little emperor, lord of all he surveys.

My throat closes up with fear. I'm late. *Late!*

The mother pushes the buggy out onto the wider pavement, and I skip round the people waiting in front of me and start running again. Alongside the hole, round the corner, down the next street.

To the traffic lights by the park – three minutes behind schedule.

Three minutes? Somewhere, somehow I have to

make up lost time. The traffic lights are red when I arrive, the cars have stopped. With a sigh of relief, I skitter across the road and into the park. Sometimes, when I've been really late, I've taken a risk and crossed roads when the lights are green and cars are racing up and down. I've discovered that I can successfully dodge moving objects if I concentrate.

The park is a short cut and there aren't many people around, so I pick up speed. It's green and beautiful and flower-filled in the summer, but now, with winter rushing upon us, the trees are stark and black, surrounded by piles of dead and decaying leaves.

I've never been here with Mum, not even in the summertime. Mum collapses with panic, struggles to breathe and sobs at even the thought of leaving the house. She hasn't been outside for seven years. The last time was just after I started school.

To the park exit – four and a half minutes. My lungs are bursting out of my chest, but I've shaved a minute off my best time. I must be getting fitter. I have three roads to cross now, and at each crossing all the traffic lights are on red and my hero, the green man, urges me to the other side before the cars set off again.

'Three times in a row!' I tell myself triumphantly. 'That's never happened before.' And it's saved me another two minutes. I'm back on schedule.

Life would be so much easier if I didn't have to go to school at all, if I could just stay at home with my mother and look after her. I know Mum wishes I could too, but she won't allow it. I worry about her endlessly when I'm away and I ring her at lunch time, every break time and between lessons if I can. She panics whenever she's left on her own.

I never know what might have happened when I arrive home from school. Mum can only walk with sticks because her legs were injured in a car accident when I was very young, but even then she can't get far without me to help her. Once she hobbled into the kitchen and tried to start cooking dinner and one of the pans caught fire. Sometimes she falls over and cuts her head or bruises herself and I find her lying on the floor in pain when I get back. She's often convinced that someone has broken into the house while I'm away; she imagines that she hears noises and it makes her sick with fear. I worry, worry, worry about her every second I'm at school.

And Mum falls apart, piece by piece, if I'm not home on time. She can't help it. Once I tripped over a broken bit of pavement and I scraped my knee and dropped my bag and everything fell out and I had to stuff it all back in – folders, books, pencil case, tissues – and then I had to run and run and run. I was nearly six minutes late that day.

Mum was crying hopelessly when I finally arrived home, and we fell into each other's arms until we'd both calmed down. That was one of Mum's Bad Days, when a cloud hangs over her so thick and black I can almost see it, separating her from me. I have nightmares about getting knocked down by a bus and being taken away to hospital and Mum not knowing where I am and panicking. I don't know what would happen then. It frightens me. I try not to think about it.

The only times I don't go to school is if Mum is having a Really Bad Day. When I skip school to stay home, I'm worried someone will notice, but it doesn't happen all that often and so far nothing's been said. No one at school knows about Mum, but my Year Group teacher, Miss Hardy, is starting to ask questions.

'Will I see your mum at Parents' Evening, Anjeela?'

'Is your mother coming to the Christmas concert?'

'Anjeela, would your mum be interested in helping out at the school car boot sale?'

'No, thank you, Miss Hardy,' I reply with the bland, bright smile I've perfected over the years when anyone asks about Mum.

I think Miss Hardy is starting to get suspicious. But it's none of her business. We're not doing anything wrong. I can manage. I can cope. I *can* look after Mum on my own.

'Do you mind this life, Anni?' Mum asks me now and then. 'It upsets me, the way you have to do everything. I know it isn't fair to rely on you so much. But . . .' Her voice always fades away, and she never finishes the sentence. Because she knows, like I do, that there's no one else. There'll never be anyone else.

'I don't mind, Mum,' I always reply. And if it

sounds like I'm telling the truth, then that's because it is how I really feel. I look after Mum and care for her, whether she's having a Good Day or a Bad Day, because she can't do it herself, and that's the way it's been, ever since I can remember.

I'm close to our house and I'm bang on time. But when I turn the corner into Pride Street, a wide road lined with big white houses and leafy, spreading trees, it's surprisingly full of people. Workmen are unloading steel barriers and yellow signs with black writing – THIS ROAD WILL BE CLOSED ON SATURDAY 8 NOVEMBER FROM 8 A.M. UNTIL 2 P.M. – from the back of a truck and there are litter-pickers and a road sweeper. Several police cars are parked by the kerb and passers-by are stopping to stare. I feel a jolt of nervousness. I don't like police or anyone in authority. If they ever found out about me and Mum, I know they would split us up.

I wonder what's going on, and then I remember hearing on TV that tomorrow the Prime Minister is visiting the new hospital not far from our house. This must be his route.

I'm so close to home I can see the red bricks of our tall chimneys just one street away in Silver Birch Lane. I feel a rush of pure relief that at least the house is still standing and isn't on fire.

I won't let all these people make me late now, not after I almost bust a lung to get here on time.

To avoid the nosy passers-by, I jump off the pavement and run along the gutter. Someone shouts out, 'Hey, you!' I don't know if they're yelling at me or not, but either way I ignore them.

To the bottom of Pride Street, then round the corner into Silver Birch Lane. The time is 4.03, leaving me two minutes to make it into the house. A perfect run.

The houses in Silver Birch Lane are even bigger and more expensive than those in Pride Street. They're screened from view, surrounded by high fences and hedges, and I don't know a single person who lives here. I've never met our next-door neighbours; I've seen them but we don't speak. People keep themselves to themselves, and I too keep my own secrets close. There are things about me even Mum doesn't know.

Our house, The Gables, is on the corner of the street. Like the others, it has a long winding drive with gates that are always kept locked, and it's surrounded by high walls so no one can see much of the big front garden with its jungle of tangled undergrowth. The house is Victorian, red-brick and gothic with twisting corridors and sweeping staircases, like the setting for an old-fashioned story about star-crossed lovers, vampires and mysterious secret rooms. It has arched windows and two attics on the top floor, one enormous, one smaller.

At first glance, the house appears very grand. But look more closely and you'll see that, as well as the overgrown garden, the roof tiles are mossy, cracked and broken, and in some cases missing altogether. Some of the windows are boarded up, and those that aren't are hidden by thick, heavy curtains that don't allow a chink of light in and are never drawn back. Ivy crawls across the red brickwork that in places is crumbling away into dust. It looks like no one lives here.

Despite it all, Mum clings to the house like a

lifeline. She worries that if we tell anyone about our situation or ask for help, then we'll be forced to leave.

'The house is the only place where I feel safe,' Mum says. She'll stay until the house falls down around us, and I'll stay there with her, right to the end. Looking at the state of the place, that time might not be very far off. My parents were wealthy before Dad died, but almost all the money is now long gone.

We never use the front door. I run down the side of the house, towards the gate into the back garden. The gate is always kept padlocked too, and the keys vanished long ago. Instead, I remove a loose board from the fence beside it so that I can slip through the gap into our huge back garden. The weeds and the grass are so high there could be a dead body lying amongst them and I wouldn't even notice. I wedge the board back into place.

Thirty seconds to go.

Now I'm at the back door. Before I take the key from my pocket, I glance around to make sure no one's watching. I always do this because Mum asked me to. She's petrified of strangers, of intruders, of burglars breaking into the house and destroying what little peace of mind she has left.

The back door is old and warped and always sticks, and the large glass panel in the bottom is missing. I've had to board it up as best as I can. I push against the door with my shoulder, hard, and, protesting loudly, it finally creaks open.

Inside, I hang the key on the hook where it's always kept, by the back stairs. Then I turn the corner and slip along the corridor, past the downstairs bathroom. I check the door. It's locked. That's how it should be. Everything is well.

Further along the corridor I stop at the next door. I don't try the handle because I know it will be locked too. Instead, I tap crisply, three distinct knocks. Our sign.

'Mum, it's me,' I call.

I hear Mum shuffling slowly across the room and then the sound of keys jangling as she unlocks the door. This is our routine every school day. Terrified of being alone, Mum barricades herself in her room, and she keeps the rest of the ground floor locked too. I leave lunch for her in her room every morning, and she only ever unlocks the door to go to the downstairs bathroom. I sometimes wonder how Mum would ever get out quickly if there was a fire. Another thing I try not to think about.

My relief that I've made it on time doesn't last long as the door swings open. Inside the dimly lit room Mum is leaning on her sticks, and I can see from the shattering pain and anxiety etched on her face that this has turned into a Really Bad Day.

Mum shakes her head warningly at me.

'Don't make a noise,' she whispers, her voice thick with terror. 'There's someone upstairs.'

Friday 7 November, 4.06 p.m.

I have two mothers.

One is sweet, kind and funny. Her jokes crack me up and we giggle together for hours. We like the same TV programmes, the same things make us laugh and cry. We love to watch reality talent shows and documentaries about animals, even with all the killing and blood and gore, and we like movies, old and new, about wizards and witches and dragons and fantastical lands. We play cards and Scrabble, although our Scrabble set is so old we've lost most of the Es and some of the As. Mum says that just makes it more of a challenge.

We read the same books that I choose weekly from the local library. We gobble up detective stories and crime stories and mysteries; we can't get enough of them. Mum insists on reading them first to check they're not too violent and gruesome for me, but she

17

knows I'm tough. I have to be. I don't know anyone else who has a life like mine.

Sometimes, when we've finished all our books and turned off the TV, my mum spins mesmerizing stories about far-off places where the red-gold sun beats down on the desert and ancient ruins lie half buried in the sands. Or she tells me about the frozen beauty of Antarctica, where icebergs float, taller and wider than our house, and sleek blue whales surface from the depths of the seas, tails thrashing against the foamy waves as they sing to each other. I know Mum's never been to any of these places, but she makes them come alive with her words. The stories become so real I can almost feel the searing heat of the sun on my face or taste the salty sea-spray on my lips. Stories are our life-line, one of the best things Mum and I can share. We love to hear them, read them, tell them.

But my *other* mother is tired and sick and unhappy. When she feels like this, which is often, she only wants to lie in bed or sit quietly without talking. Nothing in the world seems right to her. Her legs throb and ache. She sinks under the terrible pain that envelops her. She can barely eat or drink. She doesn't sleep. The thought of going outside the house makes her shake, turn white and gasp for breath.

It's my job to look after her.

I move forward now to give her a reassuring hug. 'It's all right, Mum,' I say gently. 'I'm home now. Everything will be fine.'

Mum's breathing is shallow, panicky, and she's trembling. She's tiny and dark-eyed, like me, and her hair is long and black, threaded with silver. 'It's true this time, Anni,' she whispers. 'There's someone upstairs. *I heard them.*'

'I guess you did hear something,' I agree. Mum thinks we have intruders a couple of times a month at least, and I've learned there's no arguing with her. 'But remember last time you said there were noises?' I lock my arm into hers and begin to help her back across the room. 'It was just the sound of a branch knocking at an upstairs window.'

'This is different,' Mum insists. 'I heard footsteps. At least, I *think* I did . . .' Already she sounds a little less sure of herself.

We shuffle at Mum's pace over to the sofa. Our old living room is now Mum's bedroom and living space combined. I sleep next door in what used to be our dining room. We moved downstairs permanently a little while ago because it took so long for Mum to get up the staircase to bed, even with my help. It took me months to work out how to dismantle the beds with a screwdriver, carry them downstairs, piece by piece, and then re-assemble them. Finally I had to heave the mattresses off the beds and push them onto the landing so that they slid right down the stairs to the ground floor. I told you I was tough.

The heavy curtains in Mum's room are drawn, as usual, and the TV is on but muted. It's always the one warm space in the house because Mum has an old gas fire – we can't afford to heat any of the other rooms very often. A photo of my dad holding me, just three years old, stands on Mum's bedside table, and I glance at it, gathering strength, as always, from my dad's kindly face and wise, loving eyes. My dad was many years older than Mum and he died when I was a baby, so I don't remember him much. Mum finds it painful to talk about the past so I don't question her about Dad, but I can talk to him inside my head, at least. Sometimes, when I'm stressed and can't think properly, I'll ask myself, *What would Dad do?* And, from somewhere, I always seem to find an answer.

I help Mum to sit on the sofa, once expensive cream leather, now sagging and wrinkled with age. 'I'll go upstairs and check,' I say. 'It won't take long.'

'No!' Mum clutches my hand, still fearful. 'If we stay quiet, they might just go away.'

'It's fine, Mum.' I pat her hand. I speak calmly. We've been through this so many times before. 'I'll check the traps to make sure no one's disturbed them and I'll be right back. I'll make tea and we'll talk about the weekend.'

Mum's face lights up as I knew it would. 'I'm glad it's Friday,' she says, and for the first time since I arrived home, she smiles. 'Be careful,' she calls after me. I can tell from her voice that already she's settling down, her heart isn't racing so fast, and she's feeling less stressed. All because I'm here.

I head into the hallway. The carpet under my feet

was once thick and plush, but now it's faded, worn and frayed. I avoid the worst holes, those that might trip me up, without looking down.

The front hall is large, as big as a room, the floor tiled with black and white diamonds and squares. The tiles are grimy and cracked. The chandelier that hangs overhead is also a dusty shadow of its former self, the glass droplets dulled and dirty. I check that the bolts and locks on the front door are all in place. This door hasn't been opened for years. It's probably stuck fast by now.

Ahead of me the wide, wrought-iron staircase with its torn and grubby carpet sweeps grandly up to the next floor.

I run up the stairs, avoiding the broken board halfway up, and at the top I pause and look down. The pattern of sewing threads, almost the same shade of red as the carpet so they aren't noticeable, is exactly the same as when I laid it out weeks ago. No one has passed this way and disturbed it.

I step over the threads and walk around the middle floor of the house, checking the rooms, one by one.

Some are locked and even my mum doesn't know where the keys are now. Behind each door lies antique furniture of dark wood draped with dustsheets, elaborate curtains decorated with flounces, fringes, bows and beads, richly coloured carpets and rugs woven by hand in the Far East. There are several bath-rooms with claw-footed tubs and silver taps in the shape of fishes and wall tiles painted with pearly murals of shells and long-haired mermaids, their shine now tarnished by dust and time. Every room has some kind of treasure – marble statues, oil paintings of landscapes on the walls, ancient tapestries of hunting scenes, Chinese vases taller than I am. My dad was an antiques dealer and I know some of these treasures must be valuable. But Mum refuses to get rid of any of them. And to be honest, how on earth would I go about selling them?

Carefully I check all the traps that Mum asked me to set, the ones that help her to feel safe. Buttons balanced on tops of doors and on doorknobs, scraps of paper placed carefully on windows and window-sills, more patterns of thread arranged on the floors.

Nothing has been disturbed, no doors or windows have been opened, no one has passed this way except me.

As I wander the corridors, I'm mentally listing all my jobs for the next two days. 'Get the washing done,' I remind myself. Our ancient washing machine complains loudly, but it still works – I don't know for how much longer. 'Ironing. Lots and lots of ironing. Clean our bedrooms and change the sheets. Cook stuff and fill up the freezer. Go to the supermarket and the library.'

My dad's study is at one end of the first-floor landing. I haven't set any traps here, but I always slip inside just the same, and I spend a moment or two standing silently beside the shining, mahogany desk, now covered in a raggedy old sheet. The book-lined walls are garlanded with cobwebs like silvery Christmas decorations, and I tell myself to remember to sweep them away. Occasionally, when Mum's asleep, I come here and sit in the battered leather chair and talk to Dad. Sometimes I even speak my thoughts aloud.

Now for the attics. I'm hungry now, and I'm tired because Mum never sleeps well and I got up three times to help her to the bathroom last night. But I know if I don't check the attics thoroughly, she won't settle. Even though she's downstairs, she knows exactly where I am because she counts my footsteps as I walk along the upper floors.

With a heartfelt sigh, I leave Dad's study and trudge round the corner and up the staircase to the top floor. On the dark landing there are doors to the two attics, one on each side of the stairs, both closed. The attics are empty except for a few bits and pieces. Mum told me my dad was planning to renovate them to let out to lodgers, and most of the junk was cleared out just before he died. The only thing left for me to do is pop my head round each door, so that I can tell Mum truthfully there's no one hiding there. Then I'm done.

I peep inside the smaller attic first, flipping on the light. Of course, there's no one and nothing there, except for a couple of battered cardboard boxes.

It's the same story in the big attic. It's empty except for a few boxes and my old blue suitcase. I wish I had time to flip the suitcase open and take a peek at my treasures. But I don't have a moment to spare: there's too much waiting for me downstairs. Across the rooftops I can see a row of police cars in the streetlights, and I stand and watch them for a while.

Finally, I run down the attic stairs, impatient to give Mum the good news. Everything is fine, just as I expected, just as it always is.

Friday 7 November, 4.24 p.m.

When I hurry along the first-floor landing to the main staircase, I see Mum below me in the hall. She's attempting to climb the stairs, slowly and painfully, leaning on her sticks. I fly down the steps towards her.

'What are you doing, Mum?' I scold. 'You know you shouldn't be trying to get upstairs.'

Mum's eyes flash at me. 'Just a moment, young lady,' she retorts. 'I'm the parent here, not you, remember?'

'Sorry,' I murmur as I guide her back down. Sometimes Mum surprises me. I see a spark of fire in her, a glimpse of the person she used to be. I wish I could remember more clearly what she was like before she became ill, but I was too young. Now those days are long gone and it's no use crying over things that aren't going to change.

'You were a long time, Anni – nearly twenty

minutes, and that's why I got nervous,' Mum explains. 'Did you close all the doors upstairs?' She always asks me this. The winter wind is howling and whistling through the rotting window frames even as we speak, and Mum feels the cold badly.

'Yes, Mum,' I reply, as I always do.

Outside, the darkness is wrapping itself around the house now, and raindrops are chasing each other down the windows. It's time for tea and we walk slowly to the kitchen, down the corridor on the opposite side of the entrance hall. Mum unlocks the door and sits down at the old, knife-scarred wooden table. The breakfast things are still there, plates and bowls and mugs. I didn't have time to clear them away this morning before racing off to school.

'Did you have a good day, love?' Mum asks me when I've filled the kettle. Next I swiftly remove the dirty dishes from the table and begin the washing-up.

I shrug. 'It was OK,' I reply, elbow-deep in soapy bubbles. 'Double French on Friday afternoons is a brain killer. Whoever did the timetable this year must be having a laugh.' I rack my brains to think of something to entertain Mum. 'Oh yeah, there was a Year Nine fight in the playground at lunch time.'

'A fight?'

'Yes – punches, kicks, hair-pulling, the whole deal. The head of Year Nine, Mr Connolly, had to break it up. He nearly got smacked in the face himself.'

'How many boys were involved?'

'Not boys, Mum – *girls*!' I grin at her and flip the switch on the kettle as it sings to boiling point. It's supposed to turn itself off, but it doesn't any more. 'Chelsea Maynard said something about Nikita Longden's eyebrows, and it turned into a full-on cat-fight.'

Mum looks a little shocked, and I know I've made a mistake. I don't want her worrying about me while I'm at school. I rush to change the subject.

'The police are all over Pride Street,' I go on, making tea, putting the last two slices of bread in the toaster, opening the fridge. 'I was watching them out of the attic window just now. I think the Prime Minister's car must be coming that way when he visits the hospital tomorrow.'

Mum pulls a face. She doesn't have a lot of time for the PM. 'Maybe we should invite him to tea,' she suggests. 'Let him see how the other half lives.'

There's nothing in the fridge except an empty tub of margarine and an almost-empty jar of bargain-brand jam. I scrape the margarine tub with a knife to get every last little bit, and spread it on the toast. Then I wash the plastic tub and lid and leave them on the drainer to dry. Mum likes to re-use stuff, and they'll come in useful for freezing leftovers. Nothing gets wasted in this house.

'We didn't put our bins and recycling boxes out last week, Anni,' Mum reminds me as we eat a slice of toast each. 'They're full right to the top.'

'I forgot,' I reply, a little guiltily. I have so much to do, but there's always something more. 'I'll sort them out tomorrow, ready for next week.'

I don't tell Mum that there's also tons of junk mail piling up in the front porch. Our letterbox is taped shut to stop draughts and the postie leaves our letters (always bills, nothing else) on the doormat. But other people come along and chuck take-away menus, leaflets, free newspapers and other stuff into the open porch. I try not to sigh. Something else for me to do this weekend . . .

Mum can't even finish her slice of toast. She doesn't eat as much as a bird. Her eyes look heavy and she's yawning.

'Why don't you lie down for a bit, Mum?' I suggest. 'I'll go and get the shopping. We're out of everything. And we've finished all our library books.'

'It's getting dark . . .' Mum begins, but I'm already helping her to her feet.

'I'll be quick,' I promise. 'And it's only five-thirty. It's late-night opening at the shopping centre and the library. There'll be loads of people around.'

We leave the kitchen and Mum locks it behind us, as usual.

'What time will you be home?' she asks anxiously, clutching the big bunch of keys.

I do a quick calculation in my head as I put my coat on. 'Seven-thirty,' I reply. It's no use saying *I don't know* or *About 7.30* or *In an hour or two*. Mum needs to know exactly.

I help Mum to her room, where she hugs me and then shuts the door. I hear the clanking of keys as she locks herself in.

'Don't forget to take some bags with you for the shopping,' Mum calls. 'Love you.'

'Love you more,' I call back.

Friday 7 November, 7.23 p.m.

I'm on my way home again, and I'm two minutes late. I speed up. Anxiety gnaws at my insides like a hungry rat.

The shopping took me longer than I thought, and there were queues everywhere, even in the library. The handles of my recycled plastic bags, packed to the brim, are cutting into my fingers. I try to run, but it's impossible, weighed down as I am with library books, veggies, bread, milk and everything else. I have to settle for walking as fast as I can in the freezing, drizzly rain, taking in deep breaths through my nose and panting loudly. The strong wind is battering me, tugging at my coat and trying to slow me down. But if I keep up this pace, I will just make it home by 7.30 p.m.

Even though I bought the cheapest of everything, I

still couldn't get all we needed. There was just twenty-five pounds in Mum's current account, and I didn't have the card for her savings account with me, so I could only withdraw twenty at the cash machine. All my grandparents are dead, and we don't have any other family, so it's not like there's anyone we can ask for money, so we have to be careful. I shopped at the cut-price supermarket, dashing up and down the aisles, and I borrowed six books from the library. Because of all the queues, I only had ten minutes to look around the shopping centre, gazing in windows, wandering around clothes shops, deciding what I'd buy if I had the money. I usually spend at least half an hour this way.

A police car patrols slowly past me as I hurry down Pride Street, and I keep my head turned away, moving out of the streetlights and into the shadows. I feel uneasy. Guilty. As if Social Services have sent them to capture me, put me in a home and force my mum to see a doctor.

I rush through the back door at 7.29 and counting. Dropping the bags, I lock the door behind me, throw the key onto the hook, gather up the bags again and stagger to Mum's room. I tap three times.

'Mum, it's me,' I pant. 'I'm home.'

No sounds from inside the room. I frown.

'Mum?' I tap at the door again. 'Mum, are you there?'

There's an agonizing silence. But just as I begin to panic, I hear the sound of keys clinking, and the shuffle of Mum's slow progress towards the door. It swings open and, to my horror, I catch a glimpse of Mum's fear-ravaged face. She looks a thousand times more terrified than when I arrived home from school earlier. Frantically she beckons me inside.

'Mum, what's happened?' I ask as, leaning on her sticks, she clumsily re-locks and re-bolts the door as fast as if the devil himself was right behind me.

Mum can't speak. I leave the bags lying on the floor, guide her over to the sofa and sit her down.

'I – I fell asleep.' Mum makes a huge effort to explain, even though she's shivering violently. 'I woke up – and someone was trying the handle of my door, trying to open it and get inside.'

I bite back the impatient words that rise immediately to my lips. Not again!

'It must have been a dream—' I begin, but Mum shakes her head.

'No, Anni, it was real!' she says emphatically. 'I could hear footsteps. I could hear someone moving around outside. Someone's broken in!'

I have no choice. I know nothing will reassure Mum except another search of the house.

'I'll go and check.'

Mum clutches at me. 'It's too dangerous, Anni!'

I've never seen her quite this frightened before, and I feel a ripple of unease. 'It's fine.' I try to soothe her, rubbing her back. 'You were probably still half asleep and dreamed it all—'

A loud noise from upstairs stops me in my tracks. A bang, followed by a crash. What on earth was that?

'You see?' Mum whispers in a trembling voice.

My nerves start to jangle and suddenly I'm on edge, adrenalin pulsing through me.

'It's probably just another tile falling off the roof,' I say, trying to find the most logical explanation. 'The wind's pretty bad out there.' If I let myself be sucked into the bottomless pit of Mum's fear, we'll both be done for. There'll be no escape for either of us. But I'm curious. 'I'll take a quick look.'

'Anni—'

'Just lock the door behind me and only open it if I tap three times,' I say, helping Mum to her feet. 'I'll be as quick as I can.'

At the door Mum strokes my hair and whispers, 'Take care.'

I nod and slip out into the corridor. I hear the key in the lock behind me.

The house is cold and quiet as I tiptoe along the corridor towards the entrance hall. The only sound is the roaring of my own heart in my ears. I check the front door. Still locked and bolted, no sign that anything has changed. I debate whether or not to switch on the light above the stairs, but in the end I do, and I move silently up the main staircase, eyes darting right and left, looking for signs that someone has passed this way.

Then, when I reach the top of the stairs, I see that the pattern of threads I laid out there so carefully has been disturbed.

Friday 7 November, 7.49 p.m.

Shocked to my soul, I stand there staring at the crooked threads until I almost go cross-eyed. I'm willing myself with every fibre of my being to be wrong. But the evidence is right there in front of me. Someone has crept up the staircase and, not noticing the trap, has fallen right into it.

Oh God. Mum's worst fears have finally come true. Someone has invaded our home.

What do they want? Have they come to steal Dad's antiques? Are they hiding somewhere, watching me? How am I going to protect Mum? Myself? We could be murdered in our own home, and no one will know. Our bodies could lie here undiscovered for days until someone at school finally notices that I'm missing . . .

For a moment I am nothing – not human, just a mass of raw, all-consuming fear that freezes me where I stand. I can't take this in, I can't think straight, and yet I also know, with crystal-clear certainty, that I am the only person I can depend on right now.

Instinctively I snap the light off and I swallow hard, heart racing, mind panicking, all my senses on feverish high alert. I have only one thing left to fall back on – what would my dad do, if he was here right now? He'd look at the situation calmly and try to think things through. Wouldn't he? I'm sure he would.

Then, through the fog of blind fear, a tiny doubt starts to break in. I remember that, earlier, I ran along the landing and down the stairs when I saw Mum attempting to climb up to find me. Did I disturb the threads myself without realizing? It was perfectly possible. Relief surges through me.

But what about the noise we'd just heard? I stand still, straining my ears. The house is silent as death. There's not a sound.

'Get a grip, Anni,' I mutter under my breath. 'Come on, how can anyone have broken in?' The front door hasn't been opened for years. I locked the back door when I left, and then again when I got back. All the windows have locks. There's no way to get in.

Maybe I should stop reading so many stories.

Curiosity killed the cat, they say, but I can't let this go. I have to check. I have to know.

I stand at the top of the main staircase, not daring to switch on the landing light again. Darkness wraps itself around me, scary and threatening, and yet also, somehow, reassuring. If there's an intruder here, he won't be able to see me. And I, at least, can find my way around the house in the dark. There are six rooms along the section of corridor on my left that leads to the back stairs, six rooms on my right towards the attic stairs. First, I have to decide whether to go left or right.

I turn right. Two of the rooms on this side are always kept locked because of broken floorboards. But my old bedroom is here, also the master bedroom, a bathroom and my dad's study. I'm going to search these four now, before I lose my nerve. I have to steel myself to take hold of the handle and open the first door.

My room is ghostly, silent and filthy with dust, a large space in the middle where the bed used to be, the walls pinned with torn photos of fluffy kittens, cute dogs and boy bands that split up months ago. It's like somewhere I lived in a former life.

I boldly turn on the light, but my heart is jumping with fear, my pulse skittering. There's nowhere for anyone to hide except the wardrobe. Without thinking what I'll do if someone jumps out at me, I wrench the mirrored doors apart.

No one jumps out.

I search the whole room thoroughly, from corner to corner. It takes ages, but I have to be certain. Then, clicking off the light, I step onto the landing again and move to the master bedroom next door, my parents' old room. Taking a deep, steadying breath, I lift up the dustsheets one by one and check beneath the beautiful old furniture. Again, there's no one hiding there. None of the traps I set seem to have been disturbed either.

I move on to peep into the bathroom. That's empty too. Only the mermaids swimming on the tiled walls stare back at me with painted eyes.

And now I'm beginning to question myself.

'I don't believe there's anyone here.' I whisper the

words aloud as I close the bathroom door. 'There's no intruder. There never was. No one has broken in. *Why did I think it was true?*' I've allowed Mum's paranoid fear to infect me, and I'm ashamed of myself. It's my job to keep her from becoming stressed and anxious, and I've failed, spectacularly. That noise? Like I first thought, it was probably a tile falling off the roof.

Just to reassure Mum, I'll check the attics and the rest of the rooms on this landing as fast as I can, and then it will all be over. At last the weekend can begin.

But before I've taken two steps towards my dad's study, the last room before the attic stairs, I notice that something is wrong.

Very, very wrong.

Friday 7 November, 8.07 p.m.

The door of my dad's study is open.

I never leave any doors open upstairs. I never have, not once, not ever. Mum asked me to keep them closed, always, because of cold draughts, and I don't forget. I don't specifically remember shutting the door of the study behind me earlier, but I'm sure I did it automatically. Almost one hundred per cent sure.

Which means . . .

There is someone inside that room right now, or someone has been inside that room while I was out. It's the only explanation. Fear floods through my body, and my blood turns to ice.

I flatten myself against the wall on the dark landing and I don't know what to do. Terror holds me captive in its paralysing grip, and once again my brain has stopped functioning. All my systems have shut down.

Fight or flight? I wonder feverishly if I should

escape right now, get out of the house and go for help. There are police everywhere outside, swarming all over the streets.

And leave my mum at the mercy of the intruder?

No! How could I live with myself if—?

Or I could go quietly downstairs and get Mum and myself out of the house to safety.

But cold, hard reality bites. I can't be sure that I can persuade Mum to leave, even when she discovers there really *is* an intruder inside the house with us. Is her fear of the outside world stronger than her fear of strangers in our home? I think it might be, and then we'd both be trapped.

My options seem pitifully limited. Frantic, I scramble to pull myself together and think logically.

Maybe there *was* a burglar, but he could be long gone. Maybe he fled, leaving the study door ajar, when he heard me arrive home with the shopping. He could have escaped out the back door, the way I come in and out myself, using the key I left on the hook while I was with Mum.

Maybe I didn't shut the study door after all. I

thought I did, but maybe I didn't pull it hard enough and it swung open again.

Maybe I've just been spooked by a series of coincidences – the pattern of threads, the noise, the open door – fuelled by Mum's all-consuming paranoia. These things could easily be explained away.

Maybe, maybe, maybe . . .

I have to make a decision, and there seems only one thing to do. I check and double-check that the key is in the outside lock. Then, rightly or wrongly, I push the study door open wider with the tips of my fingers and edge my way inside.

Friday 7 November, 8.12 p.m.

The darkness is thicker and more intense than out on the landing. It's suffocating. I have to fumble for the light switch, wondering what will confront me, whether I'll have time to run for my life and lock the intruder in while I go for help. That's my plan, anyway.

Click.

Light floods into the room. Relief, pure and sweet, floods through me. I am the only person in the study, and it looks exactly the same as it did a few hours earlier, cobwebs and all. But it's not over yet.

My heart beats painfully against my ribs as I twitch aside the first dustsheet to check if there's anyone hiding under the desk. I even pull out the big leather chair to make sure. There's no one behind the striped floor-length curtains, either. Then I move over to the tall filing cabinet, also shrouded in dustsheets.

A rustling noise!

I leap back in terror, clapping a hand over my mouth to stifle a panicky scream. Grabbing at the dustsheet, I fling it aside wildly and a tiny grey mouse dashes across the room and disappears through a hole in the wall.

My knees give way underneath me and I collapse onto the carpet. I sit there for several minutes until I stop shaking. There is silence in the house all around me, but outside the wind is rustling through the trees and rattling the windowpanes. The wail of a police siren in the distance almost makes me leap out of my skin.

I don't know if I can stand this any more, but there are still rooms left to search. And now it's not just about Mum's peace of mind, it's about mine too.

I slip out of the study, closing the door, and tiptoe round the corner to the attic stairs.

There, my search comes to an abrupt end.

The door to the big attic is very slightly ajar.

I can see a sliver of light in the gap.

And I can hear voices.

Friday 7 November, 8.26 p.m.

Voices.

Not just one intruder.

More than one.

All the feeling in my body has drained away somewhere and my bones seem to have turned to water. My brain refuses to compute what I'm seeing and hearing, even though the stark evidence is right there in front of me. I know I should run, get the hell out of there, but I literally can't move my legs. *I can't move.*

Suddenly I'm not tough Anni, not the strong Anni who can cope with anything. I'm just a scared kid who's way, way out of her depth, and who wants a grown-up to come along and take care of everything.

But no one's going to come, and I know it. There's only me. Me against them, whoever *them* may be.

I see a flash of silver, something long and shining in the light from the open door. Even as the thought that it might be a gun takes shape inside my head, there's a loud *bang*. It echoes around the attic and almost splits my ears apart.

Both hands fly to my mouth and I bite down on my fingers to stop myself screaming aloud. I can hear laughter inside the attic. Then, finally, my legs come back to some sort of life, and I pull back sharply round the corner out of sight.

These are no ordinary burglars. For one thing, there's nothing to steal in the attic, so why are they in there? These intruders, whoever they are, must be here for another reason. And that means they're dangerous.

Did Mum hear that bang, the firing of a gun?

Please, Mum, I think, frantic. Please, please, *please* keep quiet and don't try to come upstairs to find me. If she did, or if she started calling out for me, we wouldn't have a hope or a prayer of escaping.

And now I realize I don't have a choice. I *have* to get Mum and myself out of this house. But I know it won't be easy and I need to buy us some time. But how on earth do I do that? I'm shaking so badly that my teeth are chattering and my knees don't seem able to support my body any more, and however hard I try to pull myself together, I can't. I can't focus, even though it's never been more urgent that I think things through calmly and clearly. All I can hear is that bang ringing in my ears, a warning of what might happen if I don't get this right . . .

Help me, Dad, I think despairingly. What shall I do? What would *you* do? Help me! I picture Dad's face, his wise, intelligent eyes. He'd do his best to save me and Mum, I know that. He'd try to outwit the intruders and get us safely out of the house.

That's what I have to do. Come on, Anni, I tell myself desperately. You've read enough stories where people are kidnapped or captured and held prisoner, you've seen all the movies. You need a plan. Think!

Then, seconds later, an idea breaks the surface of my fear-crazed mind, coming seemingly from nowhere.

Dad's study. Remember just now, when I went into Dad's study? Remember, if someone was hiding in there, I was going to lock him in? And only a moment ago, I saw that the key is still in the lock of the attic door . . .

At last I have some sort of survival plan.

'Thank you, Dad.' I send the words silently out into the darkness.

Then, gathering together what remains of my courage and strength, I turn the corner towards the attic stairs again.

There are twelve steps. The darkness is lit by the yellow gleam through the gap in the door, but I know these stairs so well, like I know almost every room in this house. I know that the third and seventh steps creak and that the tenth has a large crack in the middle, so I never put my weight on it.

Numbly I begin my walk of terror.

Step one. I notice that the blue button I placed on the banisters, one of my traps, has been knocked to the floor.

Step two.

From two to four without stepping on three is a stretch, but I make it without a single noise.

Steps five and six. *Not seven*.

Step eight. As I draw closer to the attic, the voices become a little more distinct, but not much. I still can't tell how many of them are in there. I try to focus on my own silent movements as I edge closer.

Step nine.

Avoid step ten.

Step eleven. The key shines in the lock, glowing with an almost magical light that pulls me hypnotically towards it.

Step twelve. I'm now right outside the attic door. One swift, hard pull on the handle will close the door, and one turn of the key is all that stands between me and escape.

I reach for the door handle. But my sleeve – my stupid, *stupid* sleeve – brushes against the key.

It falls out of the lock and clatters onto the wooden floorboards below.

Friday 7 November, 8.34 p.m.

I turn and flee down the stairs instantly, not even bothering to avoid the tenth, seventh and third steps, hoping frantically that the sound of startled voices inside the attic is masking my retreat.

'What the hell was that?' a man's voice yells, and there's a bustle behind me, a series of bumps and bangs and curses, then the noise of pounding footsteps on the attic floor and more voices – I don't know how many – and the sound of the attic door being flung wide open with a crash.

But by this time I'm round the corner of the landing and there's only one place I have time to hide in before I'm caught: my dad's study. Quickly I fumble for the door handle, step inside and close the door behind me.

They're running down the attic stairs now – I can hear them calling to each other – but I still can't work out how many of them there are. It feels like a whole mob has invaded our home, and I've never felt more helpless and afraid in my life.

Instinctively I race across the room, lift up the dustsheet draped over the desk, pull the chair out and crawl into the dark space. One of my few memories of Dad is playing hide-and-seek, me hiding under the desk and him coming to find me. I hope and pray Dad is looking after me right now.

I pull the chair back under the desk as far as I can, right up against me, and allow the dustsheet to fall into place.

They've turned the corner now, they're outside the study door; I can hear a babble of angry, panicked voices. How many of them *are* there? It sounds like a football crowd. I curl up, making myself as small as I can, pressing myself against the back of the desk.

Don't come in. Don't come in. Don't come in.

The door opens.

I don't even dare to breathe as footsteps pad into the room. Whoever it is doesn't switch the light on, but faintly, through the dustsheet, I can see the beam of a torch being played slowly around the room.

'There's no one here.' The person speaks soft and low to the others outside the room, and it's a female voice. A woman. Unbelievable. My heart almost stops with the shock. 'I'll take a closer look,' she goes on, and that's when all hope dies and I almost wet myself with fear. There's no way she won't look under the desk. I am about to be discovered.

'No, we're wasting time!' another voice shouts from the landing. It's another woman. She's loud and screechy and angry, and her voice alone is enough to make me petrified of this faceless, furious stranger. 'Look, we've already checked the whole house,' she continues forcefully. 'We *know* that either no one lives here at the moment or they're away for a while. Why would all the ground-floor doors be locked if there was someone here? It's empty, just like Ethan said.'

Ethan who?

'What about that key falling out of the lock?' the first woman asks, and there's a cool, steely edge to her voice that sends icy chills shivering along my bones. In her quiet way, she's just as frightening as the other one.

'Oh, the key probably wasn't in the lock properly to begin with,' the other woman snaps back. The aggression in her tone staggers me. She's dangerous. 'Or maybe the lock's faulty. This house is a real dump. I bet nothing works properly.'

There's a moment of silence. Then – and I can hardly believe my ears – I hear footsteps moving away from me. Oh, thank you. Thank you.

'Let's get back to work then,' the first woman says abruptly.

Work? What work?

'Wait, something's not right here.' A man's voice again, but I can't tell if it's the same one I heard in the attic.

'What's not right?' the loud woman demands.

'I'm not sure . . .' I hear the man reply in a hesitant voice.

'Oh, for Christ's sake,' the loud woman shrieks impatiently. 'Stop being such a pain in the—'

The door closes. I can hear them leave the landing, still arguing, go round the corner and up the attic stairs. The attic door shuts behind them with a thud.

I still don't know how many of them there are. Three, at least.

But these terrifying strangers don't yet know that there's one of *me*. They believe the house is empty. So, somehow, against all the odds, I have a chance to escape.

A great wave of optimism surges through me as I crawl out from under the desk. I'm almost drunk with relief, but it's short-lived.

Now I have to get downstairs without being heard, and that's the easy part.

Then, somehow, I have to persuade my mum to leave the house with me right away.

Friday 7 November, 8.46 p.m.

As I turn the handle of the study door, agonizingly slowly, bit by bit, I wonder what I'll do if this is a trap, and they're waiting for me on the landing. But when I finally open the door and peer through the darkness, there's no one there.

On winged feet, I fly along the landing to the top of the main stairs. Above me I can hear footsteps in the attic. Who are these people, and what are they doing up there?

But this is one time I won't allow my curiosity to get the better of me. This isn't a mystery story, something I can read curled up safely next to Mum.

This couldn't be more real.

I run noiselessly down the main stairs, rehearsing what I'm going to say to Mum, planning the arguments that will make her listen to me and do what I say to keep us safe. I don't know how to break the news to her that all her worst fears have finally come true. What do I say? What will happen when I tell her we have to leave our house right away? But somehow, I *have* to get her out. Her survival is my survival.

But when I reach the bottom of the main stairs, the door of Mum's room is open, a dim light filtering out from the bedside lamp inside. Mum is standing in the doorway, leaning on her sticks, and one glance at her face tells me she already *knows*.

I run and throw my arms around her.

'I heard them, Anni,' Mum whispers. She trembles in my arms, or is it me who's shaking? I can't tell. 'I heard voices again and I was so worried about you. I was coming to look for you. I didn't dare call out in case you'd managed to hide—'

'I did hide. You did the right thing, Mum. They didn't see me; they don't know we're here. They've gone back up to the attic. We're still safe. For the moment.'

'Who are they, Anni?' Mum asks urgently. She seems to have aged twenty years since I last saw her, and she looks tinier than ever, wrapped in her baggy knitted cardie. 'What do they want? Why are they in the attic? *Who are they?*'

I lay my hands gently over hers. 'Mum.' I make her look at me. 'We don't have time for this. We need to get out of here. Now.'

Mum looks at me uncomprehendingly, as if I'm speaking a language she doesn't understand. 'Out?' she repeats. 'You mean, out of the house?'

'Yes.'

Mum stares at me, her eyes glazed with shock. I can actually see the colour in her face melt away, leaving a waxy paleness as she realizes exactly what I'm asking of her.

'Of course,' she says, almost to herself. '*Of course* we have to leave the house. We have no choice.' She stares wildly at me. 'We have to leave the house.' She chants the words over and over again: 'We have to leave the house. We have to leave the house. *We have to leave the house!*'

Mum's shaking so much she can hardly stand upright, and I'm forced to grab her arms to keep her from falling. I'm so, so scared. I've never seen her like this before.

'Mum, I'll be there all the time. Trust me, I won't let anything happen to you. They won't hear us up in the attic.'

'Anni, can't you just call the police right now and we'll wait here, inside the house, for them to arrive?' Mum pleads.

I shake my head. I've already thought of this, and I'm certain it's not a good idea. 'It's not safe, Mum. What if they find us before the police get here? It could turn into an armed siege or something . . .' Mum's eyes widen at the word *armed*, and I curse myself silently for letting that slip. 'Look, we can hide in the garden while I call for help – we don't have to go far from the house.'

To my relief, Mum's panic seems to subside a little. She nods weakly. Leaving her propped against the doorway, I run across the room and grab her big bunch of keys and also my coat from the sofa where I left it after my shopping trip. My phone is in the pocket, and once we're safely out of the house, I'll call 999. Or maybe it will be quicker if I leave Mum in hiding and run round the corner into Pride Street where the police cars are parked.

Then, linking arms, Mum and I begin to make our way down the long, dark corridor towards the front door. We can't go my usual way out through the back garden – Mum could never manage it with her sticks. And the back garden would be a scary place for her to hide in, too.

We go slowly, and at first everything is fine. Pale moonlight filters through the glass in the front door, illuminating the darkness just a little. There's no sound but the soft thud of Mum's sticks on the tiled floor of the hall. I can't hear anything from upstairs, either.

But as the front door looms up in front of us, Mum's steps become slower. And slower. Her breathing sounds shallow and too quick in my ear, and I pray she doesn't have one of her panic attacks when she gasps for breath and almost passes out.

Can she do this? I'm not sure.

We stop in front of the door. I pull my arm from Mum's and unlock the door. Then I begin to draw back the bolts. Some of them are rusty and stiff from years of disuse, and I have to struggle and tug and heave at them with all my strength.

Beside me Mum is whimpering like a frightened kitten. She is rigid with terror. As I reach for the last bolt, she begins to cry.

'Anni, I *can't* . . .'

'Mum, please,' I beg her. 'You can hide in the bushes right outside the front door while I call for help. We'll only be three steps away from the house. Please, Mum, *please*.'

Tears still stream down Mum's cheeks. In desperation, I begin to cry myself, waiting with dread to hear what she'll say.

'Open the door, Anni,' Mum murmurs, and then she sways and trembles as if this momentous decision has drained all her strength to the last drop.

The last bolt is the biggest and it's stuck fast. Cursing under my breath, I push at it, almost breaking my fingers as I attempt to slide it back and set us free.

Then . . .

Footsteps on the landing.

Beams of light breaking through the darkness of the hall.

Shouts of anger, frustration and shock.

People – four people – are running down the stairs towards us.

We're trapped.

Friday 7 November, 9.00 p.m.

Mum lets go of her sticks. They crash to the floor and she grabs at me for support. I drop the keys and we cling to each other, blinded by the lights that are being shone directly into our faces.

'Hide your faces!' one of the women is shouting as dark figures hurtle down the stairs towards us.

Bile floods my stomach. I think I'm going to throw up.

Within a few seconds, Mum and I are surrounded by four strangers dressed all in black. I can't see their faces because they wear thin knitted balaclavas with cutouts for their eyes and mouth.

They begin to talk rapidly to each other in whispers, but I'm so frozen with terror I can't take in what they're saying. It's like my brain has iced over or they're speaking a foreign language. I was wrong, so very wrong. I shouldn't have tried to get Mum out of the house. I should have called the police when I had the chance.

Mum is leaning her whole weight on me, and I'm struggling to keep myself upright, let alone her, because my knees are juddering so much. This isn't a dream. This is real. Slowly my brain kick-starts a little, and I begin to realize that whoever these people are, they're angry. They're swearing – a lot.

'What the hell are we supposed to do now?' asks the man who's moved swiftly to lock and bolt the front door again. It's the voice I heard from inside the attic. Now he stands with his back against the door, an immoveable force, jangling the bunch of keys in an agitated manner. He's big in both height and width, his voice loud and booming, and he looms like a giant over Mum and me as we shrink together in fear. I feel he could break my bones like twigs if he wanted. 'This is a *disaster*—'

'Don't hurt my mum!' I blurt out, but the only response is a terrifying silence.

'I *knew* there was someone here!' A shorter male, more softly spoken than the first – the man I heard on the landing outside the study. 'Didn't I tell you I *remembered* leaving that door open when we did our recce of the house after we arrived?'

My heart plunges as I realize that I gave myself away by closing the study door behind me when I ran to hide. He'd recalled what was bugging him, and they'd come to search the house again. Frustration ripping through me, I think how just a moment or two longer, and Mum and I would have been safe.

'I'll kill Ethan when I get my hands on him, the stupid—' That's the loud woman, and I recognize her voice with dread. She's short and square and she stands with her hands on her hips and her chin thrust forward in front of me and Mum, right in our faces like a snarling dog. She sounds beyond anger, utterly manic with fury. 'I'll *batter* him! He *promised* us this house was empty—'

'Shut up!' the other woman says, her words snapping out like a steel trap opening and closing. 'Don't give anything away. *And do not, I repeat, do not use names.*' This is the woman who came into Dad's study, shining her torch around while I was hidden under the

73

desk. She's taller than the first and more slender. From nowhere a random thought flits through my mind: I think she's from an Indian family, like me. I don't know where that came from, and at the moment it hardly matters.

'Please,' Mum begs shakily, hoarsely, gathering the courage to speak at last. 'Please, just take what you want and go. Leave us alone, *please*.'

The tall woman moves to stand directly in front of Mum and me, and the three of us stare at each other. Her eyes through the slits in the balaclava are darkest brown, almost black. They give nothing away, and outwardly she seems the most together of them all, but something about her very stillness tells me she's just as rattled as the others. She stands there silent for a few seconds as if she's sizing us up. Tension ripples around the hall like sound waves.

'I'm going to ask you some questions,' she says evenly. I wonder if she's their leader as she's taking charge and the others aren't arguing. 'Don't shout for help or make any kind of loud noise. Not that anyone will hear you, anyway. Your neighbours are too far away.'

She's right.

'Who are you?' I ask jerkily, trying to control my panicked breathing. 'What do you want?'

The woman ignores me and looks at Mum. 'Do you live here?'

'Yes.' Mum's reply is no more than a faint whisper.

'How did you get into the house?' I ask.

But she isn't answering my questions. She's still looking at Mum. 'Who else lives here?'

I jump in. 'My dad and my three brothers are at work, but they'll be home any minute.' Somehow, the lie comes out smoothly, from nowhere, even though I'm still in a state of shock.

'Oh, great!' the loud woman bursts out explosively. She's shaking her head, a fiery ball of crackling, electric rage. 'That's just great. Wonderful. Our very first chance to prove ourselves and it's over before we've even started!'

'Let's get the hell out of here,' the giant by the front door growls nervously, and my heart leaps with relief. 'I knew this was a mistake. I just knew it was all going to blow up in our faces.'

'Unless, of course, she's lying . . .' the other man says in his quiet, considered voice.

I try not to react, but I can't help blinking nervously. The tall woman doesn't move. She drills me with her laser stare. 'Don't lie to me.'

'I'm not!'

'If six people *really* lived here, there's no way we would have been informed that this house was empty.'

The loud woman groans and begins pacing up and down in an agitated manner. I can see her fists clenched inside the black gloves they're all wearing. 'Just stop messing about and tell us who lives here,' she demands. I can almost smell the aggression she's giving off like poisonous fumes, and for a second I think she's going to hit me.

'Leave her alone!' Mum cries, grasping me even more tightly. I can't support even her tiny weight any longer, and my knees begin to buckle. The leader woman bends and picks up the sticks from the floor, thrusting them into Mum's hands without comment. I move forward to stand in front of Mum, shielding her as best as I can.

'For God's sake, don't lose it,' the leader warns the other woman. Then she turns back to Mum and me. I find her calmness more threatening than the other woman's out-of-control rage. 'Let's try again. The truth this time. Who else lives here?'

This time she's talking directly to me, and I can see there's no point in lying. I already know from what they've said that someone named Ethan has been watching our house. For how long? Days? Weeks? Why? Nothing I've read has ever prepared me for being plunged into this living nightmare.

'It's just me and my mum,' I explain slowly. 'She was injured in a car accident years ago and she isn't very well. She can't walk without sticks, and she never leaves the house. Look, just take anything you want and leave us alone, *please*.' My voice trembles and I bite my lip. I'm appealing to their better nature. But I don't know if they have one.

'Christ!' the man by the door exclaims. 'This is getting worse by the second. I think we should just get out of here right now—'

The loud woman whirls to confront him. 'And

what about all the work we've done?' she spits. 'What about all the planning? We can't give it up, just like that!'

I don't have any idea what she's talking about. But suddenly, through all the terror and uncertainty, my curiosity begins to stir, as if I've just woken up from a deep sleep.

'I know all that, J—' The man swallows the end of the sentence abruptly, stopping himself from giving away the loud woman's name, I think. 'But we didn't expect *this* . . .'

I guess he means Mum and me.

'We need to think things over and decide how we're going to move forward,' the leader says. 'Agreed?'

'Agreed,' the quiet man replies. The other two say nothing but she takes their silence as agreement, even though the man by the front door is muttering darkly under his breath. I can't catch what he's saying, but I don't think he's happy. He's not the only one.

'What are you going to do to us?' Mum asks. I can hear the desperation in her voice. I know she's realized, as I did earlier, that these are no ordinary intruders; they're not burglars.

The leader does not answer. She gazes around the hall and down the corridors as if looking for inspiration. 'What's that room there?' she asks, pointing at the dim light spilling from the open door of Mum's bedroom.

'It's where my mum sleeps,' I say. 'She can't get upstairs any more.'

'Take your mum in there and sit down,' she tells me, taking the keys from the tall man.

I have no choice. I have to obey, although a tiny spark of anger kicks in at being bossed around by a stranger in my own home. Together, Mum and I begin the slow journey back along the corridor, not knowing what we're walking into. The four intruders surround us like bodyguards. Or a death squad.

As we go, the loud woman tries the handles of the other doors. 'I need a wee,' she complains. 'Is there a bathroom downstairs? And, if you live here, why are all the doors on this floor kept locked?'

'Because my mum's afraid of burglars,' I snap back without thinking.

No one says anything and my words hang in the air, thickening the tension around us.

Inside Mum's room the two of us collapse onto the sofa and hold each other close. A memory flashes into my head of Mum hugging me after a fall when I was a toddler – now things have reversed: I'm the grown-up and she's the child seeking comfort. But I'm also drawing strength from the feel of my mum in my arms, the familiar scent of her hair. We need each other to get through this.

There we sit, huddled together in silence, watching the four of them prowl the room. The tall man checks the windows are securely locked and pulls the curtains even closer together, while the leader glances around, taking in everything with a searching gaze.

'Where are your mobile phones?' she asks.

The quiet man has already spotted Mum's mobile lying on the battered bedside table and he scoops it up. The leader's gaze swivels to me.

'And yours?'

I think, briefly, of saying I don't have one, but I know they won't believe me. 'Here.' A little sulkily, I take it from my jacket pocket and hold it out. The loud woman grabs it from me with unnecessary force.

'Get a grip, for Christ's sake!' the leader snaps at her. She doesn't seem too impressed. 'Come outside, all of you. We need to talk. We've got some decisions to make.'

The four of them go out into the corridor, leaving the door wide open so that they can see Mum and me on the sofa. They put their heads together and start a heated and very intense discussion.

'Anni, who are they?' Mum whispers. 'What do they want?'

'I haven't got a clue,' I murmur, straining my ears to catch snippets of what they're saying.

Even though I haven't seen their faces, I'm beginning to notice things about them. The giant man who was guarding the front door – he wants to leave. He's nervous. He fidgets and bites his lip and gnaws at his fingernails. 'Maybe we should abort the mission,' I hear him say.

'No way!' screeches the loud woman. She's got a voice like nails scraping down a blackboard and she's one of those people who can't talk softly to save their lives. Even though the leader tells her to keep it down, I can still hear what she says next. 'It's taken months to prepare for this. Months! We've been trusted with our first mission, and we've *got* to see it through. Or what will the others think?'

The others? There are more of them? Yes. Ethan, the man who was watching the house – he must be one of them.

'We didn't know the house was occupied, did we?' the giant man snaps back. 'It makes things a lot more dangerous, especially with all those police crawling around out there.'

The loud woman jabs him in the chest with her finger. 'Are you scared?' she jeers. 'Is that why you want to leave? Why don't you ring the others and tell them—?' She *actually* says his name then, I'm sure she does, but I can't tell what it is because the other three burst into a storm of protest and drown her out.

'*No names!*' the leader snarls, flicking a glance at Mum and me. 'And keep your voices down!'

The four get into an even tighter huddle and continue arguing in fierce whispers. It all seems to come down to whether or not they decide to go ahead with their 'mission', now that they've found the house isn't empty after all.

A film Mum and I watched not long ago called *Mission: Impossible* leaps into my head. This *is* like a Hollywood film. But who knows what the ending will be? I shiver, because it is completely beyond my control.

And if they do make the decision to carry on with the mission, then where does that leave me and Mum?

Mum is thinking the same thing. 'Anni . . .' she whispers faintly, and I know what's coming next. 'Are they going to – to kill us?'

I want to lie, but I can't, not about this. 'I don't know, Mum.'

Friday 7 November, 9.31 p.m.

Hours later – it seems that way – the leader comes back into the room. The others follow. I can tell immediately from their body language that the giant is extremely annoyed. His body is rigid with anger, hands clenched into tight fists.

'This is crazy,' he says, pacing backwards and forwards. 'This will all go badly wrong. You're making a huge mistake, Sa—'

'I SAID NO NAMES!' the leader thunders. 'How many more times do I need to remind you?' She sounds like she wants to tear him apart, limb by limb. Mum and I watch in silence, pressed as close to each other as we can get. 'We're all in this together, so quit complaining.' There is silence for a few seconds and I wait with interest to see if the giant will argue with her. But he doesn't. 'We'd better sort out a rota for the work in the attic,' the leader continues. 'We'll need to change our plans as two of us will have to be on guard duty down here all the time.'

'Everything's going to take twice as long then,' Loud Woman mutters, flashing a resentful stare at Mum and me. 'Maybe we won't even *finish* by ten o'clock tomorrow morning, and then it'll all be a huge waste of time.'

Ten o'clock tomorrow morning? What's going to happen at ten o'clock tomorrow morning? *What?*

The leader is glaring at Loud Woman and I can see the dark anger in her eyes. 'Let's not give *everything* away, shall we?' she suggests in a soft, slightly menacing tone. 'We'll get it done, don't you worry.'

'I'll fetch our rucksacks from the attic,' says Quiet Man, heading for the door.

The leader nods at Loud Woman. 'You help him.'

For a moment I think she'll refuse, but then she slouches out of the room behind Quiet Man. I can tell that she's sulking. The leader murmurs something to the giant and then comes over to the sofa. Mum instinctively shrinks back, but I force myself not to.

I look her straight in the eyes, trying to read what's behind them.

'Here's the thing,' the leader says calmly. 'We thought this house was empty and now we've found out it isn't. But we've decided to go ahead anyway and carry through what we came here to do.'

'What's that?' I ask boldly, suddenly finding my tongue but knowing she's not going to answer. Alongside the fear, I'm starting to feel deep anger at the way these intruders have barged into our lives, and that gives me a just a tiny bit of courage.

'We'll be staying here tonight,' the leader goes on. 'We're taking over the large attic at the top of your house, but tomorrow morning, when we've done what we came here to do, *we will be gone.*' She emphasizes the words, speaking slowly and forcefully, and stares hard at us. 'I promise you. We shall leave in the morning. Keep quiet, don't make a fuss, don't try to escape and do exactly as you're told. Nothing will happen to you.'

Mum is too terrified to speak; she simply nods.

'All right,' I say, but I don't believe her. How can I

rely on the word of someone who's forced their way into our house and is holding us hostage? It's madness! Escape is our only option. If we get a chance before ten o'clock tomorrow morning, I will grab it with both hands.

'I need to make some calls,' the leader tells the giant. She steps out into the hall and half closes the door so we can't hear what she's saying. I guess that she's calling Ethan, whoever he is, and the shadowy 'others'.

'What happened to you?' the giant asks abruptly, out of the blue. His words jolt me out of my thoughts, but he isn't speaking to me. He's staring at Mum.

Mum looks stricken and seems unable to reply. She opens her mouth but no words come out.

'Like I said, my mum was in a car accident years ago when I was a baby,' I reply, a bit sharply, knowing that he's only asking because he's trying to find out if Mum is fit enough to try and escape or not.

But, strangely, the giant seems interested in the details. 'Pretty serious leg injuries, aren't they, huh?' he says thoughtfully. 'Did you fracture a femur, by any chance?'

'Both of them,' Mum replies faintly, obviously wishing he would stop asking questions. She hates talking about the accident and I've learned never to mention it. Mum says it's too upsetting to think about the past, about what might have been.

'Must have been complications if you're still using sticks after all this time?'

Mum nods cagily. 'Almost all the bones in my legs were crushed and splintered.'

The giant's eyes turn to me, just as I'm wondering why he's so keen to know about Mum's injuries. I mean, he can't be a doctor, can he? *Can he?*

'So you're her carer?' he says to me.

'Her what?'

'Her carer,' the giant snaps impatiently. 'You *are* a young carer, aren't you?'

'I don't know what you're talking about,' I reply, bewildered. 'I look after my mum, that's all.'

No more is said because the leader comes back into the room just then, but I *cannot* get the idea out of my head that the giant is some kind of medical person. A doctor or nurse, maybe a paramedic. But what would someone like that be doing in a situation like this? I can't believe it. And yet . . . And yet . . .

With a flash of inspiration, I realize that this is exactly what I should be doing. I need to start fighting past my own fears in order to find out everything I can about these intruders. Then I can pass it on to the police when we escape. Even if the four of them manage to get away with whatever they're up to without being caught, my information will help the police to arrest them. I've read books about people being kidnapped or taken hostage, and I know I have to stay calm and cooperate with these intruders, whatever happens. I have to build some kind of a bond. I never thought all those detective stories would be so useful in real life.

These decisions give me something to focus on; something to do instead of simply sitting here being a victim. It gives me new hope. I'm feeling calmer, my heart isn't racing quite so fast. I take Mum's hand and squeeze it and she squeezes back. *We'll get through this, just wait and see.*

I hear the upstairs toilet flushing, and then

footsteps on the stairs. Loud Woman and Quiet Man reappear, carrying four rucksacks.

'Aren't you even going to tell us your names?' I ask suddenly. I know they won't, but I have to start somewhere. There's a startled silence and I feel a stab of satisfaction that, for once, I've wrong-footed them. 'I'm Anjeela Rai, but everyone calls me Anni,' I press on. 'And my mum is Jamila—'

'Stop it!' Loud Woman throws the rucksacks on the floor and surges forward, frustration pouring out of her. It's in her voice, her eyes and every movement of her body. Mum grips my hand again painfully, and I can hear her panicky breathing close to my ear. 'Of *course* we're not going to tell you our names, you annoying little—'

The leader steps neatly between us, grabbing Loud Woman's shoulder and spinning her roughly out of the way. 'I agree we should have names,' she says coolly. 'We may as well be civilized about this. And it'll remind us *not* to use our real ones.' She gives her accomplices a sharp look. After a moment, she points to the giant. 'He's King.' She swivels towards Quiet

Man. 'He's Jack.' Then she turns to Loud Woman, who's now opening her rucksack, pulling furiously at the straps as if she's strangling someone to death. 'You can call her Queenie. And I'm Ace.'

Every moment I'm learning something new about them and how they behave with each other. King, the giant, is nervous and twitchy and full of doom. I guess he's one of those people who always thinks the glass is half empty, not half full. The other man, Jack, isn't like that. He's quiet and thoughtful and does what Ace says without complaining. I guess that, outside of this, they're close friends. Queenie – Loud Woman suits her better – is teetering dangerously on the edge. She could blow her top at any moment, and I don't want to be around when she does.

Mum's room is large, but now it feels like there are too many people in here. I watch as the four of them unpack their rucksacks. Queenie pulls a phone from her pocket. She has a Samsung – I can see the name from here. The phone cover is bright purple leather.

Right on cue, as people always do when they see someone else checking their messages, King and Jack take out their phones too. They both have iPhones, I note. King's looks new – the latest model? Jack's is older, more battered.

'Put your phones away,' Ace snaps. 'Phone signals can be traced and phone records can be used against us.' She's already realized, like me, that everything they do, everything they say, even their body language is giving us clues to who they are. She's clever. That's why she's their leader.

'I've had a text from Ethan,' says King. Oh yes, Ethan: the idiot who told them our house was empty. 'He can come and help if we need him. Jay and Martha too.'

I just manage to stop myself yelling, 'NO!' How many of these people are there? Three more invaders? Three more people crowding me out of my own home, three more pairs of eyes in hidden faces, watching my every move? But to my relief, I see Ace shaking her head.

'Tell him no,' she replies. 'We'll get it done.'

'But—' King begins.

'The more people here, the higher the risk of getting

caught. And *please* stop using names,' Ace snaps. If the atmosphere was tense before, it just got a thousand times worse.

They unpack the rucksacks. They've brought supermarket sandwiches, fizzy drinks, packets of crisps and chocolate bars. I notice a piece of paper fall to the floor as Jack empties out his rucksack. It's a till receipt and I can see the name of the shop at the top, printed in blue and green. I know he bought the food at Asda.

Ace spots the receipt and pounces on it, shoving it into her pocket. She flashes a glance at me and catches me looking, but it's too late – I've already seen it.

Queenie picks up one of the packs of sandwiches, sighs loudly and pokes Jack in the shoulder. 'Tuna!' she moans. 'I told you I hate fish, and she doesn't eat it either, idiot.' She points at Ace. 'I *knew* you shouldn't have been in charge of buying the food.'

'Guys!' There's a sharp edge to Ace's voice. 'Mind what you say, please.'

'What's the problem?' Queenie rounds on her aggressively. 'I'm only talking about tuna fish, for God's sake—'

Ace squares up to her and I see Queenie shrink back just a little. She turns and stares suspiciously at me and Mum. I show her my bland and supremely normal expression, the one I've perfected for Miss Hardy and all my other teachers over the years. Queenie lowers her voice, but I can still just about catch what she says. 'The mother looks too petrified to remember her own name right now.'

Ace's eyes flick over to me. 'I wasn't thinking about the mother.' She doesn't even attempt to whisper.

'But she's only a kid!' Queenie splutters.

'Maybe,' is all Ace replies.

I feel a flicker of unease, but that will never stop me. Fired up and alert now, I start wondering if I can somehow get an SOS message out of the house. After all, the area around our house is crawling with police at the moment . . .

The realization hits me then, like someone just slapped my face. The shock actually makes me jerk my head back in horror.

The Prime Minister is visiting our town tomorrow

morning. His car is passing near our house on the way to the hospital.

Ace, King, Jack and Queenie are here because something is going to happen at ten a.m. tomorrow morning.

Are these two events connected?

If so, how?

I'm terrified because I don't know the answer.

I can only guess.

Friday 7 November, 10.05 p.m.

I try not to show any reaction, but now that the thought has smashed its way into my head, I can't get it out again. Suddenly I can't sit still. Mum notices my restless movements and glances sideways at me. I see nervous curiosity in her eyes. Somehow I manage a reassuring smile although my heart is hammering fit to burst.

If I believe that Ace and the others are targeting the Prime Minister, then I have to accept that they are terrorists.

Vague memories of things I've seen on TV over the years come back to me. People camping outside St Paul's Cathedral in London and refusing to move, protests outside high street stores because the owners don't pay their proper taxes, students demonstrating against huge university fees. Rioting in the streets, not just in the UK but all over the world. Cyber-attacks on banks and other institutions that people consider to be corrupt. Websites leaking secret Government information, given to them by whistle-blowers.

9/11.

7/7.

But as far as I can remember, no assassination attempts on public figures – in the UK, at least.

Is that about to change?

Are Ace and the others building some kind of killing machine in our attic?

I swallow several times, trying to control my suddenly shallow breathing.

'We'll take it in turns to work, keep guard and maybe grab a bit of sleep,' Ace is telling the others. 'Right, we simply can't afford to waste any more time. Jack and Queenie, you take the first shift in here. King and I will start work in the attic.'

'Oh, but I don't want to be stuck in here with nothing to do,' Queenie whines in her grating voice as Ace and King stuff some of the food into their pockets. She's easily the most irritating person I've ever met, first prize, no question.

'Tough,' says quiet Jack, surprising me.

'Remember what we discussed earlier,' Ace warns them. Jack slants a quick glance at me and I guess that they've been told to watch out for me. It's a compliment, in a way. But it only makes me all the more determined.

Annoyed, Queenie clicks her tongue under her breath, but for once she doesn't make a scene.

'Can we move from here and sit on Mum's bed?' I ask. I have the beginnings of a plan in my head of pretending to be asleep and then, while they're off their guard, managing to escape somehow. I haven't thought it through properly yet, though.

Ace gives me a single, abrupt nod, but Mum clutches my arm and shakes her head. 'We can't go to sleep, Anni,' she says in a shaky voice. 'I *couldn't.*'

'No, we won't.' I rush to reassure her. 'But you know you'll be more comfortable with your legs up.' For the first time it occurs to me that I need to be alone with Mum, however briefly, so that we can discuss, in secret, what our next move will be.

I help Mum up from the sofa and before we're even

halfway across the room, Queenie has settled herself in my vacant seat, reached for the remote control and turned on the TV. I grit my teeth, furious at her for making herself so at home, wishing I could yell at her and make my feelings plain. But it won't do any good. I counsel myself to remain calm. I have to keep a lid on my feelings otherwise I can't think logically and clearly. But I feel like a human hand grenade that's trembling on the edge of explosion.

Mum sits down on the edge of the bed and I take her shoes off and lift her legs up onto the mattress. I settle pillows behind her so she can sit upright, and cover her with a blanket because she always gets cold. I do all this automatically because it's what I always do, but I'm uneasily aware of all four of them observing me in silence instead of looking at the BBC News on the TV. No one says anything.

As Ace and King head over to the door and Jack joins Queenie on the sofa, the national news finishes and the local news begins.

'The Prime Minister is visiting the town of Coldwater tomorrow to open the new wing of the

Fortescue Trust Hospital,' the newsreader begins.

The atmosphere in the room is suddenly alive as if currents of electricity are pulsing and crackling through it. Ace and King stop abruptly in their tracks, Jack and Queenie sit up straighter. Now no one is looking at me – their eyes have all been drawn to the TV like metals to a magnet. Even Ace, the cool and controlled one, can't help herself. They listen silently, and it's then I know, with chilling certainty, that I'm right, and whatever these terrorists are planning, the Prime Minister is the one in their sights.

At ten o'clock tomorrow morning.

I dare not glance at Mum, and all I can hope is she hasn't realized this yet. It might tip her over the edge of fear.

The newsreader moves on to a story about a fire at a local school, and Ace tosses Mum's keys to Jack. 'You'll need these,' she says. 'We'll swap over in two hours,' and then she and King slip out of the room. I hear their footsteps going up to the attic. To do what? The sheer frustration of not knowing makes my head pound with fury.

And then I remember that my blue suitcase, the one that contains all my secrets, is up in that attic. What if they look inside? *Oh, come on, Anni, get real*, I scold myself silently. *That's the least of your problems right now. They won't look. And anyway, they wouldn't be interested even if they did.*

'This house is freezing,' Queenie complains, wrapping her arms around herself. 'I'd kill for a cup of coffee.'

I see an opportunity for – I'm not quite sure what, yet.

'We don't have any coffee,' I say, 'but I could make some tea.'

Jack's obviously surprised, while Queenie looks highly suspicious, as I knew she would.

'I'll come with you,' Jack says, standing up.

'I'd better come too,' Queenie butts in and jumps to her feet.

'Ace said not to leave either of them alone,' Jack reminds her in a steely tone. 'I'll be fine.'

Queenie 'lowers' her voice, but as usual I can still hear what she's saying. 'The mother isn't going anywhere,' she mutters. 'She can't walk without those sticks and she never leaves the house anyway.'

I can't catch Jack's reply, but I realize that Queenie is already becoming less careful about guarding Mum. That fits in very well with my plans for us to escape.

However, Jack insists that Queenie stays behind and eventually, grumpily, she does. Jack and I leave together and go across the hall and down the corridor on the other side of the main stairs. I decide to use this time alone with Jack to try to get him off guard and find out a little more. I think I will be able to hold my nerve with him because he's the least scary of all of them.

Jack unlocks the kitchen door and we step inside. I'm used to the state of it, but I've forgotten how bad the kitchen must look to someone who's never seen it before. I hear Jack's sharp intake of breath and I see the room through new eyes. Old-fashioned cupboards, cracked tiles, grubby and greasy work surfaces that never seem to look clean however hard I scrub them, broken stone tiles on the floor.

Jack fills up the battered kettle. I can feel his eyes

on me as I open the ancient fridge that wheezes heavily like someone with a bad cold. Even though I went shopping earlier, the fridge is hardly full. Everything is reduced to half-price or the cheapest brand possible. I feel embarrassed, although I know it's stupid. All right, I'm poor, but at least I'm not a terrorist.

'Is this what you do every day?' asks Jack after a few moments, startling me. This is a question I wasn't expecting.

'How do you mean?' I put the milk on the worktop.

'Well, you look after your mum, don't you? Do you do everything on your own?'

'There's no one else,' I say simply, raising my voice over the loud, bubbling sound of boiling water. 'I don't have any relatives. My mum was an only child and my grandparents are all dead. That kettle doesn't work properly. It won't turn itself off, you have to do it.'

Jack flips the switch on the kettle. 'What about your dad?'

'He was a lot older than my mum, and Mum told me he didn't have many relatives either. Dad died when I was really small. I don't remember him that much.'

'What, not at all?'

'Just bits and pieces, here and there. He used to take me to the shops every Saturday morning and buy me an ice cream, I remember that.' My voice trembles a little. If only my dad was here.

'Don't you talk about him with your mum?'

'Mum doesn't like talking about the past. It upsets her. So we don't.'

There is silence for a moment.

'Your parents must have been well-off once to afford this house.' Jack doesn't add what I know he's thinking: *So what happened to all the money, and why is your house such a dump now?* Of course it isn't anything to do with him, but I decide to tell him anyway. Maybe he'll feel sorry for us.

'My dad was an antiques dealer. But then he got ill and couldn't work and he lost his business.'

'Why didn't he just sell the house?' Jack's questions are irritating me, but I try not to show it.

'Mum said he loved this house and didn't want to

lose it,' I explain. 'He cleared out the attics so he could get some lodgers in to make money. But then he died.'

'So that's why there's not much up there except a few old suitcases and boxes,' Jack comments, taking mugs from the drainer.

I am uneasy. I'm nervous about my blue suitcase, sitting there in the big attic, holding my secrets like some unexploded bomb.

'So when did your mum become agoraphobic?'

I stare at him in confusion. 'What?'

'Agoraphobic,' Jack repeats. 'Agoraphobia is a fear of outside spaces. People stay inside their homes and don't go out. I don't know that much about it, though.'

I didn't realize Mum's condition had a name. 'She took me to school on my very first day. That was just over seven years ago. She collected me for a while after that. Then she just stopped.'

'That must have been hard on you,' Jack says softly.

An emotional hurricane of memories rushes upon me. Recollections of Nativity plays and school concerts and parents' evenings, all missed. I fight the emotion down, work hard to keep my face neutral. I have to remember that this man is my enemy. I don't need his sympathy.

'She couldn't help it,' I reply abruptly. 'Anyway, the school was only two minutes' walk from here with no roads to cross, so it was easy for me to get myself there and back, even when I was quite little.'

I push aside vivid pictures of children running out of school towards the gates shouting, *Mummy! Mummy!* and waving their paintings proudly in the air. Meanwhile I was all alone with no one to meet me, trying and failing to fasten the stiff buttons on my coat.

'Didn't your teachers notice?' Jack asks, opening the bag of sugar.

'No.' I don't tell him that I learned very early on to keep myself a little distant, to merge into the background in order to protect Mum from the prying eyes of others.

'What about when you went to secondary school? What are you, Year Eight?'

Why couldn't he stop asking questions? But this was what I wanted, wasn't it? To talk?

'Seven.' I pop tea bags into four mugs. 'I started in September.'

'Well, I thought parents usually went to the school to meet the teachers and have a look around.'

I shrug. 'Maybe they do in posh schools, but mine isn't like that. It's pretty rough. There are loads of kids in my year whose parents don't go to any meetings.'

'Still, it sounds like a tough life,' Jack remarks, and something in his voice makes tears rise thickly in my throat. I'm glad he picks up the tray of mugs and nods at me to go ahead of him. That way I get a few minutes to steady myself without him looking at my face. I think, very uneasily, that Jack has learned a hell of a lot more about me than I've learned about him. He's like a snake in the grass, slithering around a subject, asking questions to throw me off my guard.

'At last!' Queenie says theatrically, rolling her eyes as Jack hands her a mug of tea. She's lounging on the sofa with her feet on the coffee table, watching TV while Mum sits silently on the bed. I feel an urge to smack Queenie's legs off the table and yell at her. Instead, I carry the tray over to Mum and hand her a cup of tea.

'Thanks, sweetheart.' Mum wraps her hands around the comforting warmth of the cup. So do I. I have my back to Jack and Queenie, and I take a risk.

'I'm going to ask if we can go to the bathroom,' I whisper under cover of the TV noise. 'Then we can talk.'

Mum nods, her eyes enormous and fearful in her pale face. But she's calmer. Now she's started to accept the situation, it will be easier for me to plan our escape.

'My mum needs the bathroom,' I say when we've finished our tea.

'Where is it?' asks Jack.

'Left out of here and just a few doors along the corridor,' I reply.

'Fine,' Jack says with a shrug. I help Mum off the bed and prop her up on her sticks and then we begin to make our way slowly across the room.

'Hold it!' Queenie jumps into the doorway to block our path. 'You're *not* going together.'

'My mum needs help,' I retort, itching to shove her aside, 'otherwise it's really difficult for her.' It's true that I usually help Mum to wash and go to the toilet if I'm at home, but when I'm not here, she has to manage on her own. I hope that doesn't occur to any of them.

'What about when you're at school?' asks Jack. The snake in the grass strikes again.

'I'm able to go to the bathroom on my own, but it takes me ten times as long,' Mum replies quietly. I'm surprised to hear her speak up for herself. But I'm glad and relieved. Having Mum onside will make all the difference when we attempt to escape.

'I'm going to check the bathroom and make sure there's no way they can get out,' Queenie tells Jack. 'There might be a window or something.'

'The window's tiny, and anyway, I've told you already, my mum never leaves the house,' I snap.

Queenie ignores me, grabs the bunch of keys from Jack and strides off along the corridor to the downstairs bathroom. I help Mum out of the room and we follow her. When we reach the bathroom, Queenie is pulling back the shower curtain and inspecting the bathtub. It annoys me.

'We won't be trying to escape down the plughole.'

Queenie doesn't crack a smile. 'I'll be waiting for you outside,' she mutters, then she stalks past me and slams the door.

I turn to Mum and put my finger to my lips. We don't speak until we've both used the toilet and flushed it.

'Anni, why do you think they're here?' she asks as I turn the taps on. I imagine Queenie outside with her ear glued to the door, and I hope the sound of running water is masking what we're saying. 'Do you think this might have something to do with the Prime Minister's visit?'

Mum is always surprising me. 'That already crossed my mind,' I confide, washing my hands, making as much noise as I can. 'I think it might.'

'It looks like they're part of some organized protest group,' Mum replies, and I nod. 'The leader, Ace, she knows what she's doing. They're well-prepared – except they didn't realize we were here.'

'But what's their "mission"?' I ask anxiously. 'Are they just trying to disrupt the Prime Minister's visit – or is it something else?'

'I don't know,' Mum says, frowning. 'Something's going to happen at ten o'clock tomorrow morning, we know that, and it depends on what they're planning to demonstrate about. It could be a peaceful protest or it could be – violent.' Her voice breaks a little, and she sounds frightened.

'Well, it can't be peaceful, can it?' I burst out before remembering I need to speak quietly. 'They've already broken the law by coming into our house and holding us prisoner!'

'But we mustn't say anything about it, Anni. We mustn't ask any questions,' Mum warns me. 'They might get angry if they realize we're on to them. Promise me you won't say anything?'

'I promise,' I agree reluctantly.

Mum is trembling and my anxiety levels soar. I *have* to keep her safe. Her peace of mind is fragile as a butterfly's wing, even in normal everyday life, and this isn't normal.

'That Queenie just gets on my nerves, though!' I burst out, under cover of the noisy cistern and rattling pipes. 'I hate her the most!'

'Anni, I think she's nervous and frightened about whatever it is they're doing,' Mum says quietly, surprising me yet again with her insight. 'That might be why she comes across as so aggressive.'

'Well, I'm *not* going to let her bully me,' I mutter, drying my hands. 'We'll find a way to escape from them, Mum. Trust me.'

Mum stares at me in shock. 'Anni, I don't think that's a good idea—'

'Mum, we *can't* just sit here and do nothing! You just said yourself, we don't know what they're planning. We might be in serious, serious danger—'

Mum is pale, but she nods, just once, and I know she's accepted the truth of what I said.

Outside, Queenie bangs on the door. 'Aren't you ready yet?' she bellows.

'Coming.' I draw back the bolt and Mum and I

shuffle out into the corridor. Queenie goes in and looks around again, checking for – what? Maybe she thinks we wrote a message on the shower curtain and chucked it out of the window.

Thank you, Queenie. You've just given me an idea.

Friday 7 November, 11.24 p.m.

The clock ticks on. Every second seems like a minute, every minute like an hour, as Jack, Queenie, Mum and I sit in silence, watching TV. Except we're not watching, not really. The film is unfolding on the screen before us, but I couldn't tell you any of the plot, I don't know who any of the characters are and I have no idea what it's called. I don't think the others know any better than me, either.

Jack unwraps a sandwich and suddenly the room is flooded with the smell of tuna.

I can feel hunger growling in the pit of my stomach, but I also know that if I try to eat anything right now, I'll be sick.

Friday 7 November, 11.51 p.m.

I can't stand this. The house is wrapped in a cloak of darkness outside, and inside I'm feeling stifled and crowded, as if I could punch and kick a hole in the wall to escape.

Hardly knowing what I'm doing, I jump off Mum's bed.

'I need some fresh air,' I say, desperate, my throat closing up like I'm about to choke. 'Just sitting here like this is doing my head in. Can't you open a window?'

'No chance,' Queenie snaps.

'Anni . . .' Mum says no more, but I can hear the plea in her voice. *Don't lose it, Anni. Don't lose it.* She puts out her hand and draws me back down onto the bed. Reluctantly I sit beside her again. I haven't even been able to put my so-called brilliant plan into action yet because I can't think of a way to do it without arousing Queenie and Jack's suspicions.

'What do you usually do at weekends?' Jack asks. I get that he's trying to calm me by starting a conversation, but I don't want to talk to him, the snake in the grass. I don't want to talk to any of them.

'Mum and I read or watch TV,' I mutter curtly. 'We play Scrabble or Monopoly or we just talk. I do my homework. Oh, and I clean the house – well, bits of it, anyway.'

'Is that your life?' Queenie asks abruptly. I glance over and see her staring at me with those dark, aggressive eyes. I imagine her looking a lot like an angry bulldog under the balaclava.

'What do you mean?'

'I asked if that's your life? Staying in and helping your mum all the time? What do you do for a laugh? Don't you go out with your mates from school or something?'

'My life is none of your business!' I yell at her, all my frustration boiling to the surface and spilling over. How *dare* she! What right does she have?

Eyes blazing, Queenie tries to leap up from the sofa,

but Jack grabs her arm and hauls her back into her seat.

'Here's a suggestion – why don't you stop moaning and do something useful – get on with your homework or something?' Queenie snaps in an intensely sarcastic voice. I can tell she's not expecting me to agree.

I scowl at her. But then something clicks in my brain, and finally I see a way for my plan to work.

'Maybe I will, but don't tell me what to do,' I snap back. I don't want to appear too keen.

I'm about to scramble off the bed again when Mum leans over and whispers in my ear, 'Anni, don't do anything silly, will you? Don't take any risks. Promise.'

'I won't,' I reply. I'm not taking a risk. My plan is foolproof.

I pick up my school bag from the floor and walk towards the table behind the sofa.

'Where the hell do you think you're going?' Queenie asks suspiciously.

'I might as well start my homework, like you said. And I need to sit at the table to write.' We lock eyes, and there's no way I'm backing down first.

'All right, but don't try anything clever,' Queenie warns me, and she turns to the TV again. I pull a face at the back of her head that no one sees but Mum. Mum even manages a little smile.

I sit down at the table behind Jack and Queenie and open my notebook. I have English and history homework and some other boring stuff. I can't see what composing a haiku or writing about the Roman invasion of Britain have to do with my present situation. But it's going to give me the cover I need.

Quickly I scrawl some notes on the Romans in Britain that I can show Queenie if she wants to see what I've been doing (and I wouldn't put it past her). Then I flip to the last page of my notebook, and I begin writing down what I've learned so far about the four of them. Anything and everything, down to the smallest detail. That Ace's name begins with *Sa*, and Queenie's with a *J*. I note down their heights and their builds and their skin colours, and that I think Ace is Asian, possibly Indian. I record how they interact with each other, the type of phones they have, even the colour of their rucksacks. I fill a couple of pages. Then, silently, I flip back to my Roman Britain notes.

Despite herself, despite wanting to keep an eye on me, Mum keeps dozing off and jerking awake after a couple of minutes. I can tell she's exhausted.

Saturday 8 November, 00.07 a.m.

Queenie and Jack begin to talk in lowered voices. I lean across the table as far as I dare, straining to hear what they're saying.

'Do you ever wish you hadn't got involved in all this?' I hear Queenie say, surprisingly softly, her voice trembling a little. Amazingly, Mum was right. I can see it now. Queenie's scared. 'God, what if we get caught! We'd get a police record, wouldn't we? My family would kill me if that happened.'

'No one ever said it was going to be easy when we signed up for this,' Jack tells her. He speaks quietly, but I can hear the same all-consuming anxiety in his tone. 'We wanted to make a difference. We *will* make a difference. If not this time, then the next, or the next. We didn't *know* there was anybody living here. We'll get it done and then get the hell out of here.'

'I know,' Queenie replies, but she sounds not at all sure. 'I keep telling myself that.'

'It'll be all right. Honestly.' Jack lowers his voice even more, but my ears are sharp and I can just about catch what he says next. 'And go easy on the kid, will you? It's not her fault that she's involved in all this. She's only looking out for her mum.'

It takes me a couple of seconds to realize that Jack's talking about *me*. I'm expecting Queenie to jump down his throat, but to my amazement, she doesn't. I see her head drop a little, then she shrugs and nods.

'I know, I've been a bit crazy,' she says apologetically. 'I'm just so nervous about tomorrow. Sorry. I'll try harder, promise.'

'I feel bad about keeping them prisoner,' Jack confides. 'Really guilty. If there was any other way . . .'

I can tell he means it, and this puzzles me. I thought I knew what a terrorist was, before this night. Someone evil. Someone who wants to maim, kill, destroy for their own beliefs. Now I'm not sure what to think. My thoughts are confused, a maze of doubt. These terrorists seem fairly – *normal*. Even Queenie, the loud crazy woman, is beginning to quieten down a bit. Can this be right? Can terrorists appear to be everyday members of society, and then be able to switch off all their feelings and emotions to become cold-hearted killers? I suppose they can, because otherwise it would be easy to spot them, wouldn't it?

I'm caught out, then, when Queenie unexpectedly whips round to check on me. 'What are you doing?' she asks nosily, but in a slightly softer way than usual.

'History,' I reply, relieved that she didn't turn round a few minutes earlier and see me noting down what kind of phone she has.

Queenie turns away. As silently as I can, I tear a blank sheet of paper from my notebook.

Help! SOS!!! I scribble on the top sheet. *Please send police to The Gables, Silver Birch Lane IMMEDIATELY.* I write the same thing on five other torn-out sheets. Then I fold each one individually into small squares. I stash them all away in the pockets of my jeans. Then I scribble a few more notes on Roman Britain before laying my pen down.

'I need the loo,' I announce.

Surprisingly Queenie doesn't moan and object. She instantly stands up. 'Do you want to go too?' she asks my mum, and I feel a stab of dismay. But, luckily, Mum shakes her head.

Queenie escorts me out into the corridor. As usual, she watches me go inside and then pulls the door to. She doesn't close it, which is annoying, but it can't be helped.

I calculate that I have two minutes, max, before Queenie starts to get suspicious. I must be quick. I climb up onto the edge of the bath and, balancing there, take one of the folded bits of paper from my pocket. Through the frosted window glass I can see the faint silhouettes of the trees in our garden and, every so often, the beam of headlights from passing cars. The police are probably patrolling the area all night before tomorrow, unaware of the drama that's happening in our house right under their noses.

I dare not open the window to throw the SOS message out, but there's a small gap between the window and the frame where the wood has rotted. Carefully I poke my message out through the gap, into the blackness of the night. My hope is that the wind will lift it out of our garden, and someone may find it and read it and take it seriously. Not very likely, I know, but it's all I have. I push the pieces of paper through, one after another, each square a desperate cry for help.

'Are you ready, Anni?' Queenie calls.

I know that any moment she's going to burst in, and I still have one square of paper left in my hand. I jump down from the bath, shoving the message into my pocket. I'm just in time. I flush the toilet and Queenie immediately opens the door.

'You were a long time,' she says, but mildly, for her.

'Sorry,' I reply, washing my hands quickly. If Queenie can be reasonable, then so can I. Two can play at that game.

As Queenie leads me, like a jailer, back to our prison, I think about those tiny bits of paper blowing around outside, begging for help, and I wonder if anyone will come to save us.

Saturday 8 November, 00.32 a.m.

We hear Ace and King coming down from the attic. They've been up there for two hours, and the time has dragged past at the pace of a lame snail. I'm sitting on the bed with Mum, curled up underneath the blanket with her. Mum's eyes keep fluttering shut but she won't allow herself to sleep. Queenie and Jack are yawning occasionally too. On the other hand, I'm wide, wide awake, despite the time, and feel like I won't be able to close my eyes and go to sleep ever again. My whole body's on high alert as I listen out for the ring of the doorbell that will mean one of my notes has been found and the police are now surrounding the house.

I try not to think about the fact that it's unlikely anyone will even see the notes, let alone read them, because it's the middle of a dark, freezing winter's night.

Ace and King appear in the open doorway. I can't see their faces, but the way their bodies are slumped and sagging tells me they're exhausted.

'Did you manage to reach the target?' Jack asks cryptically. I listen carefully for clues.

Ace shakes her head. 'It was too many,' she says. 'We're almost fifty units down. It's going to be a tough call to get everything finished. After all . . .'

'After all, we didn't know we were going to spend valuable time babysitting,' Queenie fills in.

'And how is that *our* fault?' I lash out. '*We* didn't know you were going to break into our house and take us prisoner!' Mum slips her hand into mine and squeezes it warningly.

'Cool it, Anni,' Ace says quietly. Then, to the others, 'Let's talk.' Queenie and Jack join the other two in the corridor, and they start whispering to each other. I can't hear what they're saying because of the TV.

'Try not to annoy them, Anni,' Mum murmurs, stroking my hair. 'It won't help the situation.'

'I know.' I manage a faint smile. 'It's not at all like any of the stories we've read, is it?'

'Real life can be much more scary,' Mum replies, her face troubled.

After five minutes of talking, Jack and Queenie leave and I hear them trudging up the stairs to the attic. Ace and King come in, and King crashes out on the sofa and yawns so wide I can see all his teeth (no fillings: something for my notes). For the first time, even though he's so big, he seems no more menacing than a pet dog. Looking back, I realize that he's done nothing, really, to make us think he might injure or harm us.

Yet.

Ace yawns too, sits down next to King and rubs her eyes with her fists. Her hand moves to the neck of her balaclava and I'm electrified, sitting up in anticipation because I think she's about to remove it without thinking. Ace checks herself at the last minute, but still I'm secretly triumphant. If Ace, the leader, is so stressed she's on the edge of making silly mistakes, then my time is coming.

'You know what I'm going to do first thing when I get home tomorrow?' King says, settling his head against the back of the sofa.

'What?' Ace asks wearily.

'Have a hot shower and a few beers, then chill for a couple of days,' King replies.

Ace smiles. 'I thought you had a lot of work to do?'

'I'll sort it out somehow,' King replies with a shrug. 'If we pull this off, I'll deserve a break.'

I frown, trying to get my head around this. It's clear they're not planning to go on the run. They must be totally confident of never getting caught. How can that be? Surely they must know that every police officer in the land will be looking for them?

Ace stands up, stretches as if her back's aching. She gathers up the mugs from earlier. 'Do you want tea?' she asks King, who nods.

'It might help to keep me awake,' he replies with a giant yawn. 'I've hardly slept for the last few weeks, thinking about tomorrow—' He stops himself.

'Me neither,' Ace agrees.

'Shall I give you a hand?' I'm still desperate to find out what they're up to; perhaps Ace will let something slip if I can talk to her. 'I want to make toast for Mum and me. I know it's late, but I'm really hungry.'

Strangely, it wasn't a complete lie. I'm a prisoner, but I still need to eat, drink and go to the bathroom. Life's most basic routines carry on.

'No food for me, sweetheart,' Mum says, still fighting sleep. 'Just tea.'

In the kitchen, Ace makes the drinks and I put together cheese on toast. We move around the kitchen comfortably, easily, stepping aside to allow each other to get to the fridge and the grill and the kettle. Surprisingly, we work well together.

'How did you get into the house?' I ask suddenly, a question that's been niggling at the back of my mind for the last few hours.

Ace doesn't reply for a moment. I guess she's working out whether what she's going to say will be incriminating or not. 'We found some loose planks in the garden fence to squeeze through. Then we removed the board nailed to the bottom of the back door and crawled inside that way. We put it all back so no one would notice.'

She's right, I didn't notice. I don't say anything, but I silently file the information away for my notes. They might have taken off their gloves to remove the planks and the board. There might be fingerprints.

The kettle boils.

'You all seem to be working hard up in the attic,' I say casually, grating cheese. 'Do you think you might finish what you're doing early and leave before daylight?'

Ace shakes her head.

Then this mystery *has* to be connected with the Prime Minister's visit. 'So you'll be here till ten o'clock, whatever happens?' I push.

Ace ignores me. I think about asking outright what they're planning, but it's pointless. She won't answer, and anyway, I promised Mum I wouldn't.

'I guess you must be looking forward to getting back to your normal, everyday life,' I say, trying not to sound like I'm probing for details, which, of course, I am.

Ace turns the kettle off as it pours out a cloud of steam. 'Are *you*?' she asks unexpectedly.

I'm thrown off-balance and don't know what to say for a moment. 'Well, of course I am,' I say, irritated.

'Being a prisoner isn't any fun, if you didn't know.'

'Isn't that what you are, every day?' Ace leans against the worktop and stares directly at me. Her eyes are a pure and liquid black, burningly intense. 'Some kind of prisoner?'

'No, of course not!' I won't allow her to turn the spotlight on me, instead of herself. I made the very same mistake with Jack. 'I love my mum. It's not her fault she has problems. Anyway, I was asking *you*—'

'Of course it isn't your mum's fault.' I can feel Ace is still looking at me, even though I won't meet her gaze. 'And you're a very mature and resourceful kid. But you shouldn't have to cope with all this on your own.' Emotion wells up in me, and now I want to cry. I'm furious with myself. 'Jack told me what you talked about earlier.' I stare at her in disbelief. They've been talking? About me? 'It's very worrying,' Ace goes on. 'Do Social Services know your situation?'

'No, and it's not your problem!'

'It shouldn't be yours, either, Anni,' she replies. 'Or at least, you should be sharing it with other people. You need help. Don't you have any relatives at all? It's still kind of unusual for an Indian girl *not* to have some extended family, even in the UK. I—' She breaks off abruptly, and then I know I was right. Ace is from a British Indian family, just like me. Another tiny detail added to the big picture.

'There's no one,' I say. 'Mum's told me over and over. I know it's hard to believe, but it's true.'

'How about your doctor? Can't they help?'

I shrug. 'I don't suppose so. I don't even know who he or she is.'

Ace seems completely aback. 'You've never *seen* your doctor? Doesn't anyone ever visit here to check up on your mum? Haven't you ever been ill yourself and needed antibiotics or something?'

'Mum says I had all my jabs when I was a baby,' I reply defensively. 'And I haven't needed a doctor since. I'm never ill.'

Ace starts pacing up and down, and that makes me nervous.

'Mum doesn't like doctors,' I blurt out. 'I've got the local surgery number in my phone, though, so I can call them if I need to. And the Fortescue Hospital is close by, if it's an emergency.' The hospital the Prime Minister is visiting tomorrow morning, I think, but I don't say these words aloud.

'So if anything happened to your mum, you'd be all alone?'

I am silent, uncomfortably so. Ace already knows the answer to that question. She's shining a bright, probing light into the darkest corners of my life, and it's far too unsettling.

'You said before that Social Services know nothing about you,' Ace goes on, even though I'm eyeing her sulkily now, making my feelings blindingly obvious. 'Does that mean you don't claim any benefits?'

'Of course not,' I mumble.

'So how do you survive?'

I don't really know. 'Mum tells me how much money to take out and she gives me her cards and I go to the bank and get it from the cash machine,' I reply curtly. Then I turn away and begin to make tea. I'm sending a clear message to Ace: *I don't want to talk about this stuff any more.*

'So your mum must have savings,' Ace guesses.

'Yes, sometimes she gives me her savings card so I can transfer money to her current account to pay all the bills,' I snap, not wanting to make these involved explanations, but feeling somehow compelled to explain myself and my life, to defend Mum from Ace's prying and snooping, to show her that we can manage.

I know Ace is regarding me intently. I can feel her eyes locked onto the back of my head, even though I refuse to look at her. 'What happens when those savings run out?'

I don't answer, just lift the tea tray and walk out of the kitchen. For the first time in my life, I'm beginning to wonder about these things that I've always accepted as truth, the questions I've never asked. *What if one of us was seriously ill? Would Mum let me call the doctor? How long will Mum's savings last? What will we do if we run out of money?* But I won't allow Ace to get inside my head and mess with my mind. Nothing matters except that Mum and I get out of this house safely and away from *them*.

Saturday 8 November, 00.47 a.m.

I thought that I'd successfully deflected all Ace's questions, but I was wrong, so wrong. When we're back in Mum's room, Ace opens her big mouth.

'I've just been talking to Anni in the kitchen and she says her mum hasn't seen a doctor in years,' Ace tells King. I'm beyond shocked, as well as raging mad. Why, why, *why* would these terrorists be interested in my tiny, insignificant little life?

'*What?*' King looks astounded, confused. He also looks concerned, believe it or not. But how can that be? 'You don't see your doctor?' King jumps up from the sofa, and now he's speaking directly to Mum. 'You're not having physio? Have you *ever* had physio?'

I was all ready to leap in and defend Mum, but to my surprise she speaks up for herself. 'I'm not seeing anyone,' she says curtly, and I see another flash of that inner fire, that backbone of steel that I guess was once there. And maybe still is? 'I don't like living this way. But I know I'm lucky to have Anni to help me.'

'And anyway, Mum told me there's nothing they can do,' I say, and my white-hot anger at their interference spills out into my voice.

'Anni.' King stands squarely in front of me, his eyes fixed on my face. 'There are amazing advances in medical science every day. Every single day, Anni. There might not have been anything the doctors could do years ago, but that doesn't mean there isn't anything *now*.' He turns his intense gaze to my mum and walks towards the bed. 'Things may not be as bad as they seem,' King says gently. 'There might be something that could help your situation . . .'

Mum is staring at him and I'm shocked because, somehow, she suddenly looks so different. It's as if life is fizzing through her veins, waking her up from a long, long sleep. Her eyes are feverishly bright and her usually pale face is glowing, two red patches high on her cheekbones.

'Are you a doctor?' Mum snaps at King, and

he instantly retreats, glancing anxiously at Ace.

'It's all right, Jamila,' Ace says quietly. 'Don't upset yourself. We're only trying to help, that's all.'

Mum sits up straighter in bed. 'You can help most of all by leaving our house right now!' she tells them coldly, and this time neither Ace nor King has anything to say. There's nothing they *can* say. Silently they both move away from the bed and resume their places on the sofa.

I'm amazed that Mum has finally stood up to them, but I always believed she had that other side to her, that the person she was before she became ill was still buried deep inside, and unexpectedly, out of the blue, that person has smashed her way through to the surface. I'm so proud of her I can't speak, but it shines out of my eyes as I scramble onto the bed next to her and give her an extra-loving hug.

Mum hugs me back. She's trembling, but only a little. 'It's not over yet, Anni,' she whispers. 'I want you safely out of here before tomorrow morning comes, and I'm going to think of a way to do it.'

I'm dumbfounded, so much so that I can think of

nothing to say in reply. Mum sounds focused, determined, single-minded. I haven't heard her speak that
way or use that tone of voice for years. In an instant,
we seem to have switched roles. She's the adult again,
and I'm the child. The way it ought to be, I suppose.
But it's not something I'm used to.

Ace is opening up more packs of sandwiches and
she hands one of them to King. King slips his gloves off
before taking a sandwich from the packet, and Ace
does the same. I make a mental note to watch and see
if they touch the coffee table or anything else without
their gloves on. Fingerprint evidence.

The TV is still on, and a programme that is
basically about mindless violence, girls in teeny-tiny
dresses and car chases begins. Mum no longer seems
sleepy – she's as alert as I am and I can see that she's
turning things over in her mind, assessing the
situation.

Ace looks as bored with the film as we are, and
eventually – after it drags on for nearly an hour –
she begins flipping through the channels until she
gets to the BBC News channel. They're showing news

footage from the last few days, and one of the headlines is: PRIME MINISTER TO INTRODUCE NEW BANKING CONTROLS.

'We've heard it all before,' King says, tearing open another pack of sandwiches. 'They still haven't done much about the bankers' huge bonuses and massive pension pay-offs, despite all the promises. The bankers need to be accountable for the credit-crunch recession they got us into.'

'Oh, and maybe this country would have a bit more money if we made all the fat cats pay their lawful taxes!' Ace snaps energetically. 'What about handing over some of that money to support the three-point-six million kids whose families are below the poverty line?'

When a clip is shown of the Prime Minister talking about welfare reforms, there's even more uproar. I get the feeling this isn't the first time Ace and King have debated these things.

On and on they talk, rubbishing everything the Prime Minister says, ripping him, his government and his motives apart, and pouring out opinions and statistics that directly contradict him. I am transfixed. I've never really thought much about the things they're saying, although I guess maybe I'm one of the kids *below the poverty line*. I don't understand the politics. But it sounds like they want to sweep everything away like a tsunami, and start again from nothing. It's rather thrilling, in a way. But dangerous. For me and for Mum and, very likely, for the Prime Minister.

Despite my promise to Mum, I can't stop myself.

'Are you going to shoot him tomorrow morning?' I blurt out. 'Is that what you're here for?'

Saturday 8 November, 2.11 a.m.

No one's looking at the TV now. All eyes are locked on me. I hear Mum's sharp intake of breath, and I know I've said the wrong thing.

King leaps up from the sofa and I'm frighteningly aware once more of just how big he is. 'What are you talking about, Anni?'

'Leave her alone!' Mum flings her arms around me. Her dark eyes are blazing fire as she stares King down. 'Don't bully her! She's only a *child*—'

Strangely, King doesn't seem annoyed by this. He stays where he is and simply glances helplessly at Ace.

'You're asking us if we're going to assassinate the Prime Minister, Anni?' Ace says. Her voice is calm, with no trace of tension. 'Whatever gave you that idea?'

There is silence for a long moment.

'I thought I saw a gun,' I confess. 'When you were in the attic.'

'You were wrong,' Ace replies. 'There's no gun. We're not going to hurt anyone.'

I don't know whether to believe her. I want to, but – oh, I'm just not sure.

'We're just planning something that will make people sit up and take notice,' Ace goes on. 'That's all.'

But I can't leave it. I'm still worried. Or maybe I'm just dying of curiosity. 'So what *are* you going to do?' I push for answers.

'That's enough,' Ace tells me. 'Like I told you before, it's best you and your mum don't know.'

'But—'

'We're not telling you, Anni,' Ace repeats, still calm but with just a hint of impatience. 'So leave it.'

She turns back to the TV, leaving me steaming mad with rage and frustration. I was almost beginning to – not relax with them, exactly, but I *was* feeling a little more safe. But asking me to sit here and take their word for it that they aren't going to hurt anyone?

No!

Every bit of me cries out against simply accepting what they say as the whole truth. Ace may not be lying about their mission, but the police – and the Prime Minister – might see it very differently. The four of them have already committed a crime by breaking into our house. And if . . . and if something goes wrong with their mission and the police storm our house, will Mum and I be caught in the crossfire?

I can't take such an enormous risk, knowing that the price Mum and I would pay for doing nothing could be fatal. And that means we still need to get the hell out of here, whatever Ace says, whatever I believe.

I think about the notes I sent spinning out of the bathroom window into the darkness, and at last I acknowledge that no one is going to find one, read it and take it seriously. Those three simple steps now seem wildly unlikely. I imagine the notes floating uselessly across the garden, getting wedged in the long grass, never even making it to the road beyond.

It's time for Plan B.

I wish there was a Plan B.

'I've been thinking,' Ace says suddenly to King.

'You know how we're so far behind with the work in the attic? Maybe we only need one of us on guard down here.'

I feel Mum's fingers curl around my hand and squeeze it tight.

'Sounds like a plan.' King finishes off a Mars bar and leaves the wrapping on the table. He still hasn't put his gloves back on. I think, I need to get hold of that wrapper. Fingerprints. DNA. 'Let's see what the others think. They should be down in a minute to switch over.'

Sure enough, about ten minutes later we hear footsteps on the stairs. But it's only one person coming down. Jack comes into the room, beckons to the others, and then retreats into the corridor to whisper with them. I wonder if their 'mission' has hit a snag or a glitch.

'Anni.' Ace comes back to the open doorway. 'We need your help.'

I'm stunned into silence. Unusual for me, I know.

'What for?' Mum quizzes Ace fiercely.

'We need to open a window upstairs on the next

floor,' Ace replies. 'It's locked and we can't find the key.'

Mum clutches my arm. 'I don't want Anni going anywhere without me!'

'I'll be fine, Mum,' I reassure her, wanting to go, wanting to see if I can find *any* clues to what they're up to. 'I'll only be a minute.'

Jack stays behind with Mum while Ace and King escort me from the room. I don't understand the look Jack flashes at me as I go past him. Concerned. Anxious. What is his problem?

I walk upstairs to the first floor, Ace on one side of me, King on the other. I'm not expecting a trap. But that's exactly what it is.

Queenie is waiting for us at the bottom of the attic stairs. At her feet is an open suitcase, my old blue suitcase that I keep in the attic, far away from prying eyes.

I realize, as shame and dread and rage flood through me, that they have uncovered my secret life.

Saturday 8 November, 2.21 a.m.

Guilt and intense embarrassment settle like an unbearable weight on my shoulders. So, like a wounded animal, I turn on my tormentors and come out fighting.

'How *dare* you go through my private things!' I grind the words out from between clenched teeth. I'm desperate to scream and holler furiously at the top of my lungs, but I'm afraid, so afraid, that Mum might hear me. And what would I do then? Mum would be shocked and disappointed in me if she ever found out what's been going on, and I would be crushed. 'You had no right to even *touch* my suitcase, never mind open it!'

For once, Queenie is taken aback by my blazing aggression. 'I was just interested,' she blurts out. 'It's the only thing in the attic apart from some cardboard boxes full of rubbish. I wondered what was in there, that's all.'

'No, she shouldn't have opened it.' Ace speaks calmly from behind me. Wild-eyed and trembling, I spin round to face her. 'But it's done now.'

Ace kneels down on the carpet and takes a shiny, sparkling bracelet of pink and purple stones from the large pile of bangles, beads, necklaces, earrings and hair ornaments in the suitcase. She holds the bracelet up, its price tag dangling on a string. But I know how much it cost without looking: £4.99. I know the price of every single item in the suitcase. 'Where has this stuff come from, Anni?'

All the fight drains out of me in an instant. I sink down onto the bottom step of the attic stairs and cover my face with my hands. Ace wants to know the answer to the question I've been dreading. I don't want to tell her, and I don't *have* to tell her, even though I know they've already guessed. I can deny everything if I want. I don't owe them an explanation, I owe them less than nothing.

But I feel an overpowering sensation of turmoil inside me, a tornado of repressed emotions being unleashed. While I hate their interference, I can't stop the urge to let it all out, to confess everything.

'I stole it.' I don't recognize the sound of my own voice. 'All of it.'

'When?' Ace wants to know.

I have to swallow two, three times before any words come. 'When I go to the library or to buy food. I always leave time to look around the shopping centre. I can't afford to buy anything, so I steal it. But I never take anything very expensive . . .' As if that made it all right. *Grow up, Anni*, I tell myself harshly. *Face it. You're a thief.*

'And you can't use them because your mum would notice,' Queenie fills in. 'So you keep them here and look at them from time to time. You just like having them. It makes you feel better.'

Queenie has nailed how I feel; she completely gets it. I'm burning up with shame and my skin is prickling with heat and my hands are still over my face so I don't have to look at her or Ace or King. I nod, just once.

'That figures,' Queenie says in the quietest voice I've ever heard from her. 'I did the same.'

My hands fly away from my face and my head snaps up at that. I stare at her in disbelief. 'You . . . ?'

Queenie doesn't look at any of us. She stares past me out of the window, and there is a long silence. 'My parents split up when I was thirteen,' Queenie replies abruptly. 'And I—' She stops, clears her throat, and I can see the sheer, naked pain in her eyes. 'I didn't handle it very well. I fell in with some kids from school who went shoplifting every weekend.'

I can tell from Ace and King's sudden stillness that this is all news to them. Me, I'm hanging on Queenie's every word.

'What happened?' I want to know.

Queenie shrugs. 'I got caught and the police were called.' At her words, I'm plunged into total fear and I start to shiver violently, as if the temperature's suddenly dropped below freezing. This is my worst, my most frightening nightmare. That I am caught stealing and Mum finds out and my life comes crashing down around me. Mum is sent to hospital and I'm put into care because there's no one to look after me –

all those terrible things that go through your head at three a.m. when you can't get to sleep.

So why do I do it then? You can ask the question, but I can't tell you the answer. I don't know why.

'Did the police call your parents?' asks Ace.

'Yes. You don't want to know the rest.' Queenie is curt, almost aggressive again, but I can see it's because she's struggling with her emotions. 'The fallout, my parents' reaction – well, it wasn't something I ever want to go through again, even though I never got a police record. It made the divorce situation a million times worse.' Her voice is bleak, and there's nothing we can say. 'You don't have to listen to me, Anni,' Queenie continues softly, 'but you should think about stopping this before it ruins your life. And it could. Believe me.'

'I don't know why I steal!' The words explode from me like a bullet from a gun into the silence that follows Queenie's confession. I wasn't even aware that I was going to say anything until the sentence was already out there. 'I don't know why I do it. I'm not that kind of person – really, I'm *not*. I know the difference between right and wrong. I *know* I shouldn't be doing it. But you're right, I like *having* this stuff. I like *looking* at it. I can't explain . . .'

I feel tears trickling down my face and it shocks me. Truthfully, I'm disgusted with myself.

'Please, don't tell my mum . . .' I gulp.

Ace sighs. 'We won't tell her.' She speaks quietly, but even my hyper-sensitive ears can tell she isn't judging me. Instead, Ace sounds sympathetic. Sorry for me. 'But, Anni, this goes way beyond that. You're living with enormous stress every single day.' She searches my face with her clear gaze, and I can see compassion in her eyes. 'You cope brilliantly, we've seen that, but somewhere, something's got to give.'

'Ace is right,' King says. He is brisk and practical, but in a kind way. I'm dazed, wondering if I'm hearing things. This isn't at all what I was expecting. 'You're managing fine at home, and we've seen how much you help your mum day by day. But the shoplifting – well, I'd guess it's perhaps a symptom of your hidden frustrations boiling over every now and again, given the day-to-day stress you're constantly dealing with.'

King speaks with authority, as if he knows what he's talking about, and although I'm still shaken and ashamed, I am now able to look him in the face as I take in every single word he says. 'You're using every coping strategy you can think of, right or wrong, to get through each day as it comes.'

What he says is so close to how I secretly feel inside, how I've been feeling for years, that my tears are unstoppable. They flow faster, and I sniff and swallow and try to stop the sobs. I don't want Mum to see me with red eyes. How could I explain?

'You need help, Anni, and you need it soon,' Ace says. 'Yes, there have been lots of cuts made to the welfare budgets, but there's still support available out there.' She smiles wryly at me. 'You can't go on like this, and you shouldn't. You really shouldn't.'

'It's totally worth getting your mum to see a doctor too,' King advises. 'She has some range of movement, and it's possible that new advances in medical science could help her become a little more mobile. I'm . . .' He hesitates, glances at Ace. 'I'm – um – involved in the medical profession, and believe me, whatever diagnosis your mum was given at the time of her accident should be reviewed. There might be something doctors can do to make her life easier, and yours too.'

'Now we'd better get on,' Ace says matter-of-factly, snapping the suitcase shut.

'Thanks,' I whisper, wiping my face. I can't say anything more because I'm still reeling from what just happened and my head is spinning with unanswered questions. I wonder yet again why I've never talked to Mum about the way our life is. Why have I just accepted it all? Do Mum and I really have to exist this way? Could there be an alternative? Perhaps there might be. But will Mum feel the same?

'Three of us will work in the attic, and one will stay with Jamila and Anni from now on,' Ace tells Queenie. 'You go down and sort out a rota with Jack.'

'I'll carry on working with you two for a while,' Queenie decides.

Ace and King head into the attic and Queenie escorts me back to Mum's room. We don't speak. I've just shared my darkest secret with these people, and their sympathy has disarmed me. There's so much for me to think about. Like, what am I going to say to Mum after they've left? Can I persuade her that life could be so different – better – for both of us if we take our courage in both hands and face our fears?

Saturday 8 November, 2.45 a.m.

Queenie and I go downstairs, and Queenie begins to explain the new, three-person rota to Jack. Mum doesn't notice I've been crying, and as soon as she sees me she begins to pull herself up off the bed. 'I need the bathroom, Anni,' she says directly.

Queenie returns to the attic and Jack, who is left on guard, escorts us to the bathroom. He allows us to close the door. There, thrown together in that small space, I look closely at Mum. Her whole face is even more alert and alive than earlier. I haven't seen her look this way for years. What's happened?

'Anni, I have an idea,' she whispers, her voice overflowing with suppressed excitement. 'I've thought of a way to get Ace and the others to leave the house. Now, before daylight comes.'

It's a huge effort for me to drag my thoughts away from my conversation with Queenie, Ace and

King, and focus on what Mum has just said.

'What do you mean?' I ask, confused.

Mum turns on the taps, full blast. Then she takes my wrist and pulls me closer. 'Upstairs, in the little attic, there's a secret cupboard,' she gabbles into my ear under cover of the rushing water. 'Well, it's not really a cupboard; it's a safe, a hidden safe. But it's big enough for someone small to hide in. My idea is this – if you go and hide in that cupboard, Ace and the others won't have a clue where you are. They'll think you've escaped and gone to raise the alarm. All right, so they'll search the house and the gardens, maybe they'll even go out into the streets, but if they can't find you . . . !'

I don't say anything because I'm struggling to take in what she's telling me.

Mum rolls her eyes in frustration. 'Don't you *see*, Anni? If they can't find you – and they won't because they'll *never* guess there's a hidden safe – they'll panic and leave the house! They'll want to escape before the police get here!'

'A hidden safe? A secret cupboard?' I repeat, still in

something of a daze. I wonder if Mum is feeling quite all right. This is real life, not an Enid Blyton story. 'In the little attic? Are you *sure*?'

Mum is nodding impatiently before I've even finished speaking. 'It's hidden behind one of the panels between the wooden beams,' she explains, the words tumbling out of her in one long stream, without pause. 'Your dad had it built years ago to store valuables, but I think you'd be able to get inside it. I've been racking my brains for ages wondering if there was somewhere in the house where you could hide yourself away, and then I remembered the cupboard!' She's flushed with triumph. 'I haven't been up there for years, but I can tell you exactly how to find it—'

'Mum, wait!' I interrupt, not sure whether I'm coming or going. This so-called *secret cupboard* is impossible to believe in. Especially as I'm struggling to cope with my mum's apparent personality transplant at the same time. 'Mum, let's think about this logically. Even if there *is* a hidden safe in the little attic—'

'There is,' Mum replies. She's so confident that,

finally, I grudgingly accept it, however unlikely it sounds.

And now I'm caught, well and truly caught, in a trap of my own making. I can't tell Mum that my feelings about Ace and the others are beginning to change. The only way to convince Mum, by telling her how kind they were to me just minutes earlier, involves having to confess to being a shoplifter, a thief. Not that. Never that.

But on the other hand I know Mum's right. We should still be trying to escape. Once again I wonder what might happen if the 'peaceful mission' turns bad. If things go horribly wrong. And besides, it's just not me to do what I'm told and sit around waiting until morning, even if I don't think Ace and the others mean us any harm. I make a lightning decision. I'm going with Mum and her plan.

'All right, well, we still have several problems, Mum,' I say, frowning. 'For one, how am I going to get up to the little attic while we're being guarded? And even if I *did* make it up there, don't forget I'll be right close to where they're working – they're almost *sure* to hear me. And besides—'

'I know what you're going to say,' Mum interrupts. 'You don't want to leave me behind on my own.'

I nod.

Outside, Jack taps on the door. 'You all right in there?' he calls.

'Just coming,' I reply.

'I want to keep you safe, Anni,' Mum whispers fiercely. 'We have no clue what's going to happen, and I'm so afraid you might get hurt. Ace and the others – they're dead set on this mission, whatever it is. None of us knows how all this will end, not even Ace.'

'I don't think they'll hurt us, though,' I say confidently. 'I think Ace was telling us the truth.'

'So do I,' Mum agrees. 'I'm guessing they're just four ordinary people who've got themselves mixed up in a situation they can't get out of. But they'll only get more exhausted, edgy and nervous as the clock keeps ticking towards ten a.m.,' she adds softly. 'Their behaviour could change. They might become threatening as they get more and more stressed.'

I am silent. Mum sounds so convincing, as if she really knows what she's talking about, and I can't argue with her reasoning. These are all thoughts I've already had myself, and I know she could be right. Everyone has their breaking point. I'm becoming certain now that her plan is still our only sensible option, despite what just happened upstairs.

'Anni, I want you to do this,' Mum says resolutely. I can't remember ever seeing her this way before, so focused and determined. She's like another person. It's exhilarating but, strangely, it's also kind of scary. 'It's our last chance. And now that only one of them is guarding us, we have to go for it. And if their "mission" backfires, I don't want you anywhere near it. I *have* to protect you, my darling. And this is the only way. Will you try? Will you go and find the secret safe?'

'Yes,' I whisper as Jack knocks on the door again.

'Brave girl!' Mum gives me a brief, loving squeeze. 'Listen to me carefully, Anni. When you get to the little attic, look for the third panel on the left and push it hard on the right-hand side. The panel swings out and there's a space behind it. That's the hidden safe.'

Slowly she reaches for the bolt. 'We're coming,' she calls to Jack.

'But how am I going to get upstairs without being seen?' I ask urgently.

It appears impossible, but Mum already has some kind of a plan. 'Wait until I lie down to sleep and then say you need the bathroom,' she murmurs, and there's no time for more because she's opening the door and there's Jack, probably wondering why we've been so long.

Silently I follow Mum out into the corridor. She seems to have a plan for everything at the moment. I'm not used to her taking charge. It unnerves me slightly.

I wonder if Jack will notice this change in Mum; her new-found confidence and determination. It seems so glaringly obvious to me. But Mum puts on the acting performance of her life as she trudges along the corridor, leaning on her sticks, head down, radiating weakness and defeat. She even pretends to trip at one point and I grab her arm.

'Thanks, sweetheart,' Mum says. 'I don't know what I'd do without you.' She sounds ill and feeble and nothing like the cool, level-headed woman issuing instructions in the bathroom just moments before. I'm filled with admiration and respect.

Back in our prison cell Mum settles down on the bed and I sit next to her, as usual. Jack flips through the TV channels and finds an old black-and-white movie about the Second World War. I pretend to watch, but Mum's instructions run through my head on a never-ending loop: *Wait until I lie down to sleep and then say you need the bathroom.*

Tensed like a cobra about to strike, I'm on full alert. Meanwhile, Mum calmly gathers a book from her bedside table and begins to read. I'm surprised, but then I understand and silently call myself every kind of an idiot. We can't put Mum's plan into operation yet. It would look too suspicious. We only just got back from the bathroom! *Wait, Anni. Wait.*

I pick up my own book. It's about a girl who's trying to find her missing sister, but I can only pretend to concentrate. I can't take in a single word.

Half an hour later I feel Mum moving restlessly beside me.

'Anni, I don't feel so good,' she murmurs, laying down her book. 'I'm tired. Really tired. I don't think I can stay awake any longer.'

I'm quivering with anticipation, but I manage to stay downbeat, keep my voice normal. 'Well, we don't usually stay up so late,' I say pointedly, so that Jack can hear. 'Why don't you try and sleep for a bit now?' I suggest.

Jack doesn't even glance away from the TV as Mum lies down and closes her eyes. I tuck the blanket around her and can't help but admire her acting talent once more. Mum doesn't rush it, doesn't overdo it. She tosses and fidgets for a good ten minutes before finally relaxing and seemingly falling into an utterly realistic doze. Her breathing is deep and even. She deserves an Oscar for this performance.

If Mum can do this, then so can I.

I don't rush, either. I turn the pages of my book while I count up to five hundred inside my head.

Saturday 8 November, 3.23 a.m.

Four hundred and ninety-eight.

Four hundred and ninety-nine.

Five hundred.

'Sorry, Jack,' I say casually. 'I need the bathroom again.'

He glances over. 'No problem,' he agrees easily.

I'm somewhat stunned. Jack isn't going to allow me out of the room on my own, is he?

'Should I wake my mum up?' I ask, and then could have *kicked* myself black and blue. But I don't really understand Mum's plan. What is she hoping? That I'll be allowed out of the room on my own? Or maybe she thinks Jack will leave me in the bathroom and return briefly to check on her – perhaps she's planning to call out or distract him in some way – giving me time to make a run for it up the back stairs.

Jack looks over at my mum. 'No, let her sleep,' he says kindly.

'Can I clean my teeth and wash my face while I'm in the bathroom?' I ask, hoping to buy myself just a little extra time. 'There isn't much space when Mum and I are in there together.'

'Sure,' Jack replies. He accompanies me across the room and then stations himself in the doorway. 'I'll wait here,' he tells me. 'I can watch both of you this way.'

He can too. But he doesn't. Jack's enjoying the film and he can't stop himself glancing over at it – the lure of gunfire and Nazis chasing escaped prisoners of war around the countryside. As I walk down the corridor towards the bathroom, I don't look back, but I can see Jack's reflection in the chipped gilt mirror, heavy and antique, that hangs on the wall ahead of me. He isn't watching Mum, he isn't watching me. He's staring at the TV.

I take a risk and grab what is surely my one and only chance. The bathroom is to my right, but I don't go in. Silently and swiftly I whisk past the closed door round the corner, and then I press myself against the wall out of sight. My heart is fluttering like a giant butterfly trapped inside my chest as I wait for Jack's cry of surprise, the sound of his footsteps pounding along the corridor to recapture me.

But I hear nothing. Jack, still watching TV, thinks I have gone into the bathroom.

How long do I have before Jack's suspicions are aroused and he comes to find out where I am?

I glance at my watch. Five minutes or ten? Maybe less?

Saturday 8 November, 3.25 a.m.

I kick off my shoes. Then silently I fly up the back stairs on bare feet, avoiding the holes in the carpet that's even more frayed and raggedy than the main staircase. In just a few seconds I arrive at the next floor. Now I have to make it along the corridor to the other end of the house in order to reach the attic stairs. This means I shall have to pass along the top of the main staircase without making a sound.

I creep along the corridor as fast as I dare. I try to breathe slowly and deeply, but I can't control the loud, panicky beating of my heart and it sounds like a thunderous roar, bouncing off the walls and echoing in my ears. I can't believe Jack won't be able to hear it. Then, as I near the head of the big staircase, I am racked with indecision. Jack is almost directly below me now. Should I slow down and pick my way steadily, carefully across the top of the stairs, ensuring I don't make a single sound? Or should I just run for it?

I run. There's not really a choice because I don't have the luxury of time. Noiselessly I scoot across the top of the stairs, every moment expecting to hear a shout, a yell.

Nothing.

Once again I check my watch and see that only two minutes have passed, even though I feel like I've aged several years. Already I'm at the bottom of the steps that lead up to the attics. Now to get past Ace, King and Queenie.

The light above the stairs has been left on so at least I can see where I'm going. Once again I remind myself of the sequence of steps. *Avoid the third, seventh and tenth.*

And now I'm on the landing, right outside the big attic, and the only thing that's separating me from discovering their mission is the closed door. I should pass quickly into the smaller attic before I betray myself with one small sound.

But I can't.

I stop and listen. There's nothing except a faint, strange noise, like the rushing of the wind. Ace is talking, but I don't know what she's saying. Queenie replies in her normal ultra-loud voice, but even then I can't make out any words. I strain to work out what's happening, dying to put my ear against the door, which would be madness. I don't have time for this.

Reluctantly I turn away.

The door to the smaller attic stands ajar and I slip easily through the gap. It's so dark I can see nothing, and the dust is already catching at my throat as I close the door quietly behind me. I pray I don't start coughing and give myself away. Even though the attic windows are thick with grime, there is enough light from the moon, the streetlamps and the headlights of passing cars, including the occasional blue flash of police lights, to see what I am doing.

The attic has wooden beams in the walls that slant this way and that, and between them are white-painted panels. There's nothing in the room except a few empty, battered cardboard boxes and lots of dust.

Look for the third panel on the left and push it hard

on the right-hand side. The panel swings out, and there's a space behind it. That's the secret safe. Mum's words swim into my head and I swerve away from the door and head to the wall on my left.

Third panel between the beams. Right-hand side. It's easy to find.

Now, push, Anni! Push!

I push with all my strength, but nothing happens.

I try again. And again. Then again and again, with growing desperation, feeling my way up the side of the panel, pushing hard every few centimetres. But I know I'm just pushing against plaster and solid brick, and sickening frustration overwhelms me. Mum was wrong. There's no secret safe here. I wonder uneasily if my mum is all right, or if her mind is wandering off along some track that isn't quite normal . . .

But she was so sure.

I take a step back. Maybe Mum's memory has dimmed over time? Maybe the panel opens differently? I check all around it, pushing experimentally at the other three sides, but nothing moves under my probing fingers.

That's it then, I think, defeated and disappointed, and I wonder if I'll have time to get back downstairs before Jack realizes I'm not in the bathroom after all. But then I take a step back, and this time I survey the panels on either side of the one Mum told me about. The panel on the left looks just as solid and unyielding, but the one on the right, the fourth panel along – is it my imagination, or does it look very slightly different to the others, one of the upright edges sticking out just a little too far? You wouldn't notice unless you were looking for it.

Hope floods through me, making my hands tremble as I reach out and push the edge of the panel. This time there's an almost instant give under my fingers that makes my heart sing. Just a little more effort and then – well, it's like something out of *Indiana Jones*.

The panel swings slowly and pivots. One edge moves inwards and the other outwards, revealing a dusty space under the sloping eaves behind it. I get a real head-rush of triumph and delight, intoxicated by my success against all the odds. I peer inside the safe and I can see it's quite a narrow space. There's not much room to stand upright. In fact, there's not much room at all because the cupboard is stacked with boxes and boxes of papers, yellowed with age and curling at the edges.

I don't have time to stand around patting myself on the back, though. Another glance at my watch now tells me that I've been gone for nearly six minutes. How much longer before Jack comes looking for me?

I try squeezing inside the cupboard, but there are too many boxes and not enough room for me. Mum must have forgotten that Dad hadn't got around to clearing it out. Swiftly and methodically I begin to move some of the boxes out, concentrating on not making a sound. They're full of paperwork, boring stuff like bank and credit card statements addressed to Rajveer Rai, my dad. I place them near the other empty boxes, hoping Ace and the others have never looked inside the little attic, and if they have, that they don't remember how many boxes were there before.

I grab one more box from right at the back of the cupboard, and instantly feel the bottom flaps give way. Cursing under my breath, I hold it together underneath until I can lower it noiselessly onto the attic floor. A few bits of paper have fallen out of the bottom of the box, and I leave them, turning away, but one of them is a photograph and it catches my attention.

I scoop the photo up, though every nerve is screaming *Leave it and get inside the cupboard!* But I can't because I've already recognized my mum. It's a photo I've never seen before. She's wearing jeans and a black T-shirt with a yellow happy-face logo, and she's standing on a bridge – somewhere in London, I think, because I can see St Paul's Cathedral in the background. I can hardly believe it's her, she looks so different, and it's not just because she's younger and her hair is longer. It's her face. She's laughing; she's beautiful and glowing and alive. She looks confident enough to conquer the world.

And she's not alone.

Mum's holding hands with a young man. It's not my dad. I don't know who he is – an old boyfriend, maybe? I've never seen him before, and yet I feel a flash of confused recognition, as if he's someone I might have met, once upon a time.

Saturday 8 November, 3.35 a.m.

I know I must hide. I've been gone more than ten minutes. Jack's going to find out any second now that I'm not where he thought I was. But I can't tear myself away from that photo.

I turn it over. On the back is written: *Jasmine and me, 2000.*

Jasmine?

My mum's name is Jamila.

Questions are tumbling quickly through my mind, too confused for me to pinpoint clearly, and I want answers – but to what, I'm not exactly sure. I can't help myself. I know I shouldn't, but I kneel down and open the flaps of the collapsed box.

There are no bank or credit card statements inside. Instead, I find a jumble of photos, newspaper clippings, letters and what I think are old-fashioned computer disks. I don't have time to read anything through, because I'm in real danger of discovery any moment now, but still I can't tear myself away. I leaf through the contents of the box, unable to make any sense of anything.

Another photo, this time of a Sikh wedding.

I've never been to a Sikh wedding. I've never been to any wedding, ever, but I've seen pictures and read about them in books at primary school. The bride wears a red *lengha*, shimmering with golden embroidery, and matching gold jewellery – long earrings, armfuls of bangles, a ring on every finger attached to delicate chains that meet at her wrists. Her hands are painted with intricate patterns of henna.

That's what my mum is wearing in this picture.

And the bridegroom? He wears a dark suit and a red turban. I can see that the man marrying my mum is not my dad.

The bridegroom is the same man from the first photo.

Saturday 8 November, 3.37 a.m.

Who is this man?

Why has my mum changed her name?

'Ace! Anni's gone! *Ace!*' Jack's voice pulls me sharply out of my bewildered daze. He's shouting frantically as he runs up the stairs from the ground floor. Then I hear the door to the big attic being flung open with a crash as Ace, Queenie and King dash out and run down the stairs.

I scramble to my feet, all confusion cleared, my mind sharpened by an instant rush of pure panic. The four of them are yelling at each other and so I can clearly hear what they're saying.

'What do you mean, Anni's gone?' Ace demands angrily. 'You were supposed to be watching her!'

'She said she needed the bathroom,' Jack gabbles, out of breath. 'I waited in the hall, by the door to her mum's room. After ten minutes, I banged on the door, then I opened it and she wasn't in there—'

'And you've left Jamila on her own as well!' King yells.

'I locked the door behind me. I'm not *that* stupid—'

'We don't have *time* for this!' Queenie howls. 'Let's just find Anni before she gets out of the house somehow and calls the police!'

'She might have gone already,' King points out. I can hear the tension in his voice, taut as elastic pulled tight.

'How?' Queenie demands. 'We have the keys to every door and window!'

'All right, this is what we'll do . . .' Ace begins issuing instructions, but her voice is getting fainter as they move further away from me. No one has thought to check the little attic because they don't think there's anywhere to hide in here. They're searching the other two floors first, and if they do decide to check the attic, I'll already be concealed inside the secret safe.

I tiptoe across the dusty wooden floor, leaving the box of secrets behind me. I can't think about it now. I tell myself there must be a reasonable explanation for those photos, even if nothing comes to mind. Anyway, I have more important things to concentrate on right now. Mum's relying on me, and it actually looks like her plan is going to work.

I slip inside the cupboard. I can just get inside without ducking my head, but the sloping roof means I can't stand upright without stooping slightly. Never mind, there are still boxes left that I can sit on. And I'll stay here as long as it takes, until Ace, King, Jack and Queenie have fled the house, assuming I've gone to raise the alarm because they can't find me. I hope Mum is still pretending to be asleep, and that she stays safe.

Now I'm inside the cupboard, all I have to do is push the panel back into place from this side. I'm a bit nervous about whether I'll be able to get out again, but logically I realize all I'll have to do is push the opposite edge to make it open. And even if I get stuck, I mustn't panic. When Ace and the others have finally gone, Mum will come to look for me if I don't appear. It will take her ages to struggle up two flights of stairs with her sticks, but I know she'll come . . .

All the time I'm telling myself these things, I'm pushing on the panel, trying to close it. *It's not closing.* It's not even moving. Frustrated beyond imagining, I grit my teeth and put my shoulder to it and heave and shove, but still it's not budging. It only occurs to me much, much later that maybe it's not possible to close it from the inside, maybe there's some kind of safety feature to stop a person getting trapped in there.

If I can't close it – and I can't – then I have no hiding place. When Ace and the others eventually search this attic – and they will – they'll see this open panel right away.

I need another plan. Something, anything, but I don't know what.

I run out of the cupboard and stare wildly around the attic as if someone's going to pop up and yell, *Here's your escape route, Anni! Come this way!* But of course there's nothing but bare floorboards and card-board boxes and dust.

A tapping sound filters into my consciousness. I tiptoe across the attic towards the window and pull back one of the curtains. Outside, in the darkness, I can see the big oak tree that stands just outside. It's the tallest tree in our garden, with branches spread far and wide, and the tips of some of them are brushing against the cracked glass.

I could throw out the last note I have – it's still in my pocket. Then a fully-formed, and much better, plan leaps into my head. Open the window, climb down the tree, escape out of the back garden and, instead of just hiding away, actually go for help.

It's risky and dangerous, especially in the dark, and Ace or one of the others might spot me as they search the house, but I have nothing left. I can't let Mum down. I need to make her plan *work*.

In an instant I'm across the attic, lifting the handle and pushing the window open. Now, close up, I can see how rotten and warped the wooden window frames are. Water has seeped through the damaged wood and sits in puddles on the windowsill. I guess this is because of the constant *drip-drip-drip* of rain-water from the broken guttering around the roof.

I climb onto the sill. I thought I'd get through the

window easily, but it's a tight fit. I undo the handle and allow the window to swing outwards freely, as wide as it will go, to give me more room. And poking my head outside to assess the situation, I try not to worry about the fact that the tree seems further away from the window than it first appeared. It's stopped raining now, and the wind has dropped a little, but there's still an icy breeze shaking the branches of the oak tree. I hesitate, realizing how perilous my plan is. Then I think about Ace and the others running around the house, searching frantically for me, I think about Mum praying her plan will work, and that makes me strong. I'm going to get us out of this.

I can already see that the branches closest to the window are little more than twigs, and won't be enough to bear my weight, even though I'm small and slight. But if I can just reach a little beyond them, there are thicker branches that I'll be able to grab onto.

Maybe.

I have to try.

I grip onto the top of the window frame with one

hand, and then I slide my body through the open window as far as I can until I'm crouching on the outside sill. I'm right above the cracked patio of paving slabs a very long way below me, my only anchor my left hand clinging grimly to the inside of the window frame. *Don't look down, don't look down.* Then, steadying myself, I lean forward as far as I dare and try to grab hold of one of the bigger branches.

They're just out of my reach.

Groaning under my breath, shivering with terror yet sweating heavily, I make another attempt. But it's no use. I'm too far away. I have to think again.

There's only one thing I can do. It's even more dangerous, but I'm doing it anyway.

I slide back inside the attic and I pull the window in a little, slipping the handle back into place so that the window stays open as far as it can go. I test the handle several times, making sure it doesn't move. This is the only thing that's going to stop me crashing down onto the hard, unforgiving paving slabs below me.

Then, somehow, I have to get outside again through this narrower opening. It's a struggle, but I manage it, wriggling through until I'm sitting on the windowsill outside, legs dangling in thin air. And now, with a leap of faith, numb with fear, I lean forward and grab the top of the open window. Then – not thinking, not planning, just doing it – I launch myself off the sill into space.

I've done it! I've done it! I'm clinging on tightly to the top of the open window, hanging from it, my legs swinging below me. I've made it! I'm heady with victory, thrilled with my success. Already I can see that I'm much closer to the bigger branches of the oak tree, as I knew I would be – all I have to do now is let go of the window with one hand and stretch across the space to grasp one of the branches. That's all I have to do . . .

The sound of creaking, cracking, splintering wood is like the sound of someone crying out in pain, as if the house is calling a warning to me. Suspended from the window, I'm transfixed for a moment as triumph melts away and is replaced by terror. Oh God, the window is falling apart under my weight! Desperate, I reach for the tree, but it's already too late. Inside the attic, the handle has torn away from the rotten wood of the window frame and it's now flapping uselessly around, not able to hold the window steady and in place. The window, with me hanging from it, opens wider and wider, swinging me away from the oak tree and towards the solid wall of the house. I shut my eyes tightly and pray that it doesn't bang against the brickwork, crushing my fingers.

The window stops a little way from the wall, and then begins swinging gently to and fro in the breeze. I realize with cold, sharp clarity that somehow I have to get back into the house; I'm too far away from the oak tree now to think about escape.

Wheezing and panting with effort, I attempt to lift one of my dangling legs and hook it sideways over the windowsill, hoping to pull myself and the window back towards the attic and safety. It's so incredibly difficult. My arms are taking all my weight and my muscles have become a mass of burning flesh.

Then all hope is lost as, with shrieks of protest, the window itself begins to collapse. It tears itself away from the hinges at the top of the frame with creaks and groans, and swings crazily away from the house, with me still clinging helplessly to it. Now only the bottom hinge is holding the window in place, and it's the only thing stopping both me and the window from falling like stones onto the hard ground beneath.

I don't want to give up, but I know when I'm finally beaten.

'Help!' I shout as loudly as I can. My voice is weak and faint at first, but becomes stronger as I realize that if no one comes *I'm going to die*. 'Help! Help me!'

Saturday 8 November, 3.53 a.m.

No one is coming and I'm in agony, my arms feeling like someone is trying to rip them off my body.

Then there is another shriek of splintering wood as the window is torn further away from the frame. *Don't look down.* But I do look down, I can't help it, and I see myself lying there on the patio, twisted and broken, and I close my eyes.

Saturday 8 November, 3.54 a.m.

Footsteps, I hear footsteps! I hear people running up the attic stairs!

'Help me,' I gasp.

I'm too far away to see into the attic, but I manage to turn my head. Just seconds later the light is switched on and then Ace looks out of the window. She curses under her breath and I can glimpse my own fear and panic reflected in her eyes.

'Hold on, Anni!' she tells me. 'We'll get you safely inside.'

But the window lurches again as the bottom hinge protests, and I'm tipped sideways, further away from the attic. Ace and the others won't be able to reach me now. Then I feel the soft, rotten wood under my fingers begin to crumble into dust, and I know it's all over. Once again I close my eyes. *Goodbye, Mum. I love you.*

'Anni!' Ace shouts. 'Anni! Look at me!'

There doesn't seem to be any point.

'ANNI!' Ace roars.

At last I open my eyes and slowly turn my head.

Ace is half in, half out of the window, straddling the sill with her legs. It's no use, there's nothing she can do. I've already said my goodbyes and given up. But then something happens I'm not expecting.

Ace pulls off her balaclava and tosses it onto the floor of the attic.

Instantly I'm woken up, as if from a trance or dream. I snap back to full consciousness, shivering, unable to believe what I'm seeing.

'King and I will grab you while the others hold onto us,' Ace tells me. She's outside the window now, sitting on the sill and moving herself along it to get as close as she can to me. The breeze is ruffling her dark hair, and I can't take my eyes off her face. Ace is so pretty, beautiful even. I never pictured her like this. And she's young, much younger than I ever imagined. Nineteen? Twenty? Unbelievable.

'Anni, do you trust me?' Ace asks softly.

'I trust you,' I whisper as King also clambers through the window. Straddling the sill, he grabs Ace's hand. Someone – Queenie or Jack, I can't see which one – has their arms around King's waist and is clinging onto him.

'I'm going to lean out and grab the window, and then between the four of us we'll swing it back towards the attic, Anni,' Ace says, as matter-of-factly as if she's asking whether I'd like a cup of tea. 'Ready?'

I give her one shaky nod. Now I'm not just terrified for myself, I'm frightened for Ace as she reaches forward, trying to grip the window. The only thing keeping her from falling herself is King's hand in hers, and, I guess, Queenie and Jack bracing themselves inside the attic. And the sill she's sitting on isn't solid either – the wood is rotting away there too.

Somehow, Ace has managed to get a hold on the window. My heart is almost bursting out of my chest by this stage.

'Now!' Ace yells. 'Pull!'

For a heart-stopping second or two, nothing happens. But then, after what seems like a hundred years, I feel the window slowly begin to move. Ace, King, Queenie and Jack are using all their combined strength to pull the window towards them, back to the attic, and me with it. I can hear them grunting and groaning with the effort it's costing them. *Hurry, hurry*, I plead silently. *I don't know how much longer I can hang on.*

I'm almost there. I can see inside the attic and there's Queenie with her arms tight around King, and Jack, in his turn, holding onto her. A human chain. And then – and then – I feel King's free arm round my waist. He hauls me towards him onto the sill and, finally feeling safe, trembling with relief, I let go of the window.

King pushes me unceremoniously through the gap into the attic, and I tumble heavily onto the dusty floor. I lie there for a moment, breathing shallowly, fully aware of what might have happened to me, and the realization numbs my entire body and I can't move. Shaking uncontrollably, I watch as Ace wriggles her way back along the windowsill, and then she and King are pulled into the attic by Queenie and Jack. It's then I notice that the bottom hinge, the only thing keeping me and the window from crashing to the ground below, has almost torn away from the frame. A few more seconds and I would have been gone.

Ace sinks onto the floor as if her legs won't support her, and the others do the same. All of them are breathing heavily.

'Are you hurt, Anni?' asks Ace in a low voice. I can't speak so I just shake my head and stare at her face. Her dark eyes and long lashes, wide mouth and white teeth – I could see all these before, but now I can also see her heart-shaped face, her small nose and creamy, pale brown skin, the dark, glossy hair. Never in my wildest dreams did I ever imagine Ace looked like this.

'God, if anything had happened to you, Anni—' Ace begins. She has to stop because of the emotion in her voice. I can see the terror in her eyes as she remembers what just happened, and I begin sobbing with sheer relief that I've survived.

Queenie has her head in her hands and she's shivering violently, making whimpering noises. Then I realize she's crying too. Jack slips his arm around her.

'It's OK, Jess,' he murmurs.

'It would have been our fault,' King says starkly. He climbs to his feet and begins pacing up and down. 'If something terrible had happened – it would have been our fault!'

'It wasn't meant to be like this,' Jack mutters, resting his head against Queenie's. I can hear the anguish in his voice.

'In a few hours we'll be gone and you'll never see us again, Anni,' Ace says, her eyes locked on mine. 'That's the honest truth. It isn't worth risking your life. Do you believe me? Promise me you won't try anything crazy like that again?'

'I promise,' I whisper, gulping back tears, and I mean it. 'Thank you.' At last my breathing has calmed and I can finally force out the words I should have said five minutes ago. 'You saved my life.' I turn to Ace. 'I'd given up until you took your balaclava off. I know why you did it. Thank you.'

Ace shakes her head. 'Don't thank me,' she replies in a low voice. 'I feel guilty enough as it is that you and your mum got dragged into all this.'

'If we didn't have other people relying on us, we'd have been out of here like a shot,' Jack states. 'We'd have left straight away when we found out someone was actually living here.'

'You see, we've been planning this for ages,' Queenie adds, still sniffling. She's trying to wipe her eyes, but her balaclava is getting in the way, and suddenly, like Ace, she rips it off, pulling it over her head with one swift movement.

My first reaction is – *Queenie's not much older than me!* She only looks about seventeen. She has cropped, bright pink hair and seven hoops and studs in each ear. I gaze at Queenie's face and I see resolution and determination and courage. She looks like some-one you could trust, someone you could rely on at all costs.

'Is this a good idea?' King asks nervously, looking from Ace to Queenie.

Ace shrugs. 'I don't know,' she replies. 'Probably not.'

Silence for a few seconds.

'Oh, what the hell,' says Jack suddenly. 'I'm sick of wearing this thing.' And he too recklessly whips off his balaclava. Unlike Ace and Queenie, Jack looks exactly as I expected him to. His face is kind, open and honest, there are laughter lines around his eyes, and he looks safe and dependable with that quiet, unshowy strength that's always drawn me, however reluctantly, to him. But, like Queenie, he doesn't look that much older than me. Seventeen? Eighteen maybe?

'I think this is madness,' King says quietly. 'But we're all in this together, so . . .' He rolls his balaclava up over his head and removes it. His features look finer, more clear-cut, without the mask. And his hair is long, longer than Queenie's, and a dark chestnut brown. He's a little older than Jack, but still, like Ace, I don't think he's more than about twenty years old. He's far too young to be a qualified doctor. I guess, from what he's said before, that maybe he's a medical student.

The relationship between us has shifted, changed, transformed. I honestly don't feel afraid of them any more. How can I, now that I can see them all as they really are? Looking at their faces, whole and unmasked, is like finding the missing pieces of four jigsaw puzzles and slotting them into place. They're not evil. I truly believe that. I know I should be memorizing their faces, storing up details for the police, but I'm not sure it's what I want to do. I know I should, but it all seems too much right now.

'What's that?' Jack hauls himself to his feet. I look where he's looking and realize that he's staring at the secret safe. The panel is still stuck open where I left it. 'Is it some kind of hidden cupboard?'

'Mum said it was my dad's safe,' I tell him. 'The plan was for me to hide there so you'd think I'd escaped, and then you'd leave. But I couldn't close it from the inside. That's why I tried to get out of the window.'

Jack goes to see, and King joins him. They push the panel into place and out again, commenting on how clever it is. Now I'm reminded of what I found in the cupboard. With an uncomfortable feeling of dread that I can't explain, I turn slightly to look at the card-board box sitting on the dusty attic floor with its mysterious photos and newspaper clippings and computer disks.

'What's the matter, Anni?' Ace asks. She notices the look on my face straight away, and I wonder at her – what's the word? – intuition, that's it. She's alive and sensitive to how people are feeling. A fleeting thought crosses my mind: I wish we could be friends. But that can't be possible.

'I found that box.' I point to it. 'It's got some pictures – and – and family stuff in it that I want to look at. But I don't want my mum to know.'

Ace studies me without speaking, just for a moment, and I think she guesses something's going on, but she doesn't ask any questions. I like her more and more.

'All right, I'll bring it downstairs for you,' Ace suggests.

'Thanks,' I whisper. 'Be careful, though. The bottom of the box is falling apart.'

Ace nods. 'Guys, see if you can find something to board up that window,' she tells the others as she replaces her balaclava. The others do the same. I hate to see them disappear behind the black masks again, but I guess they don't want Mum to see their faces. Because of what she might tell the police? But will we really go to the police when all this is finally over? Won't it be like a betrayal? They just saved my life, after all. But I wouldn't have been trying to escape if they hadn't held us prisoner! And yet they've been so very, very kind to me . . . Oh, I can't think about this now.

Ace scoops up the box. 'I'll take Anni back to her mum and take the next watch,' she says, and Jack hands her the keys.

Ace and I are silent as we go downstairs. She leaves the box on the table by the front door, and although she throws me a quizzical glance, she still says nothing about my strange request.

My mum's heard footsteps and she's sitting up, no longer pretending to sleep, and struggling to reach her sticks. Her eyes are full of hope that drains instantly when Ace and I come into the room.

'Sorry, Mum.' I rush over to her. 'I found the safe, but once I was inside, I couldn't close it.'

Mum looks at me, then Ace, then back to me.

'Never mind.' She draws me into a hug. 'You did your best.'

'Anni did more than that,' Ace speaks up. 'She tried to climb out of the attic window to escape, and she nearly got herself killed.'

Mum clutches me tightly to her and seems unable to say anything for a moment. 'Anni . . .' she croaks at last. 'Is this true?'

'Yes, but Ace and the others saved me,' I explain. Mum claps her hand over her mouth. 'If it wasn't for them, I'd have fallen, and—' An image of the unyielding concrete patio, way below my helpless, dangling body, swims into my head and I shiver in Mum's arms. 'I just didn't want to let you down.'

'Anni, you've never let me down, not ever,' Mum says firmly. I think of the old blue suitcase and the piles of cheap, shiny jewellery and I'm ashamed. One day, when all this is over, I *will* tell Mum everything. We shouldn't have secrets from each other, should we?

But . . . *Jamila or Jasmine*?

'Look, in a very short time we'll be gone,' Ace says quietly. 'In just a few hours' time we'll be out of your

208

lives and you'll never see us again. I've told Anni this and now I'm telling you, Jamila. It's just not worth the risk.'

Mum gulps several times. 'Thank you,' she whispers.

I stay still and safe in the circle of my mum's arms, but my mind is racing. Why does my mum have two names? What will I find inside that box when I have the chance to examine it properly? Will it be something exciting?

Dangerous?

Life-shattering?

Saturday 8 November, 4.16 a.m.

The minutes tick by and all I can think of is that box sitting waiting for me in the hall. I want to know what's inside. The few photos I've seen have already robbed me of my peace of mind. What else is hiding in there? I'm curious, but there's a sick feeling deep in my stomach.

Mum is exhausted and now she can't stop herself from falling asleep. I lie, tense and rigid beside her, breathing deeply, pretending to be fast asleep myself. At last I think Mum has dozed off, and it's safe to leave. But when I attempt to slide noiselessly out of bed, Mum stirs and grips my wrist. 'Where are you going, Anni?'

'Nowhere,' I reply quickly. 'Just turning over.' And we have to start all over again. The room is lit only by the TV, and Ace is still on guard, silent and watchful on the sofa.

Saturday 8 November, 4.59 a.m.

I awake with a start when I realize that someone is gently tapping my arm. It's Ace, crouching down next to the bed. I hadn't even realized that I'd fallen into a doze. Ace points at Mum, and I can see she's now sound asleep. I glance at the alarm clock. It's almost five.

This time, when I slide out of bed, Mum doesn't wake. She doesn't move a muscle. I'm so quiet I don't even let myself sigh with relief. I just smile at Ace, glad that she understands how important this is to me.

Ace doesn't say anything. She simply follows me out into the hall.

'What do you want to do with the box?' she whispers.

I hesitate, thinking it through. 'I'll look at it here, in the hallway,' I decide. 'Then I'll hear if Mum wakes up and calls for me. I don't want her to know what I'm doing . . .' My voice tails away. I could easily ask my mum why she has two names, instead of all this cloak-and-dagger stuff. And yet somehow I can't.

Ace collects the box and lays it on the hall floor. I sit beside it and open up the flaps.

'Do you want me to stay?' Ace asks quietly.

'I – yes, please.'

The two photos I looked at before – my mum wearing the happy-face T-shirt and the wedding – are on top of the pile. I plunge my hands into the sea of paperwork and search through the newspaper clippings and all the other stuff. I can't focus on those – I'm only interested in *pictures*. Hard evidence. Impatiently I spill the other things out over the carpet in untidy heaps. Ace is staring at the papers and computer disks, and I can see the curiosity in her eyes.

'Can you help me sort it?' I say, still poking through the box that seems, like Mary Poppins' bag, to have no end.

Ace nods and begins leafing slowly through the newspaper clippings, sorting them into date order. Meanwhile, I've discovered a treasure trove. There are masses of photographs underneath all the papers, and I seize on them like a starving animal pounces on prey. I drag them out of the box and study each one minutely in turn, as if they're hiding some sort of clue. I'm convinced that they are.

There are lots of old photos of people I don't recognize. The people in the pictures are mostly Indian, although some are white. Then I spot a face I *do* recognize. A little girl, four or five years old, sitting on a pink bike, and I can tell it's my mum. What's puzzling, though, is that she's with three young boys, all older than her. They can't be her brothers, because Mum told me she has no family left. Her parents are dead, and she has no brothers and sisters. So who are they?

I don't exactly know when I realize that Mum has been lying to me. It's not like a flash of lightning. It's more of a slow, confused journey towards the truth as I sift through the heaps of pictures. The three young boys appear with Mum in photo after photo, lots of them, along with a man and woman who can only be their parents. *My grandparents*. Maybe they are dead, but my mum's three brothers too? It's possible but, surely, unlikely? There are pictures of the boys as teenagers, again with my mum, in hideous 1980s fashions, and at least two of them got married, with all the family, including my mum, present. I have the proof here, in front of my very own eyes. So why did Mum tell me she was an only child?

My head is now exploding with questions that keep multiplying, and I can't find any answers. The more photos I look at, the more downright bewildered I become. Here's my mum again – beautiful and full of life, just like she is in the London picture. But this time she's wearing a flowing black gown and a square black hat, the clothes students wear at their degree ceremony. I didn't know Mum had a degree. I didn't even know she'd been to university. But here she is, standing on an old stone bridge, with green lawns and ancient buildings and a river behind her with people in punts. Oxford or Cambridge? I'm not sure, but this isn't my mum. It can't be. It's just someone who looks like her. And yet, logically, I know it *is* Mum.

I've only ever seen one photo of myself as a tiny

baby. Mum has it in her room. I'm about two months old, lying on a soft white blanket embroidered with bouncing bunnies. But here's another. It's that man again from the London picture and the wedding picture, the same man, and he's holding me. I'm wrapped in the same fleecy blanket but he's turning my face to the camera, and I know it's me. My mum stands alongside him, and they're both smiling. Like proud parents. But he isn't my dad, he's not the older man whose picture stands in my mum's room, the dad who died when I was tiny, the dad I talk to when I need someone to help me.

Who is he?

'Anni.' Ace taps my hand. 'I think you should look at this stuff.' She waves a sheaf of newspaper clippings at me. 'These articles are all about an environmental protest group called RAIDERS. I've vaguely heard of them before, when I was younger, but the group doesn't exist now. They broke up after something really terrible happened . . .'

I have to drag myself away from trying to make sense of the mystery that surrounds me. 'So?' I ask.

I'm really not interested in the clippings that Ace has organized into neat piles.

'RAIDERS was all about environmental and green issues,' Ace goes on. 'Pollution, global warming, deforestation, endangered animals, whale-hunting . . .'

Terrible as all these things are, none of them concerns me as much as my own life right now.

'Ace, I—'

'Wait.' Ace speaks swiftly, economically, knowing that my attention is already turning back to the photos. 'Let me explain what I've just been reading. The group originally called themselves Radical Eco-Freaks, but it got changed early on to RAIDERS. According to these articles, the group started in the late 1990s, and it was pretty hardcore. They were always dreaming up brilliant publicity stunts to get people talking. One of them actually managed to climb up Nelson's Column in Trafalgar Square to protest about the destruction of the rainforests, and he stayed up there for four days; it was all over the news. I'd forgotten, but now I remember seeing it on TV when I was a little kid—'

'Look, I don't want to hear this,' I break in impatiently.

'It seems they were one of the first protest groups to use new technology to get their message across,' Ace continues as if I haven't said a word. 'They started email campaigns to communicate with each other and with people all over the world, before email was really widely used, which meant they managed to stay one step ahead of the authorities. Some of the stuff they did was borderline illegal, including computer hacking, but they were totally committed to their causes. Until something went horribly wrong, and people were killed . . .'

'What has this got to do with me?'

Ace stops talking. There is intense sympathy in her eyes as she passes me one of the cuttings.

Another picture in smudged black and white newsprint. It's the same as the colour photo I've just seen of me as a baby with Mum and the mysterious man. Underneath, the caption reads:

LAWYERS KANVAR AND JASMINE KAPOOR, FOUNDERS OF THE ENVIRONMENTAL GROUP RAIDERS, WITH THEIR BABY DAUGHTER, ANJEELA.

Silence.

'This isn't true.' My voice appears to belong to someone else who's standing a very long way away. 'This man isn't my dad. My surname isn't Kapoor. It's Rai. My mum's not a lawyer. She doesn't have anything to do with this – group. She couldn't have. I don't understand.'

For once Ace seems at a loss. She doesn't know what to say. Someone else speaks instead.

'Anni?' Mum is standing in the doorway of her room, leaning on her sticks. 'What are you doing?'

Saturday 8 November, 5.31 a.m.

There's so much I want to say, to shout even –
questions, statements, accusations – but the words
won't come. I sit there dumbly, holding the picture Ace
has just given me. Mum stumbles forward slowly, sees
it, and her expression changes to shock, horror, guilt.
She turns deathly pale, as if someone has pulled a thin
white veil across her face. Then she begins to hyper-
ventilate.

'Ace, she's having a panic attack!' I gasp, scram-
bling to my feet.

Ace leaps into action. She guides Mum, gulping for
air as she struggles to breathe, back into her room and
sits her down on the sofa.

'Breathe, Jamila,' Ace urges her. 'Slow, deep
breaths. Relax. It's OK. Just breathe.'

I watch in silence. This is usually my role; this is

what I do when the panic attacks come. But this time I can't. How can I help Mum when I'm so angry and confused I feel like battering down the walls around us with my bare hands?

Saturday 8 November, 5.36 a.m.

Gradually Mum's breathing becomes slower and more regular. I stare at her. I love her, I know I do, but I'm closer to hate than I've ever been in my life before.

'Anni.' Mum can hardly get her words out. 'Where did you find that box?'

'In Dad's safe,' I reply shakily. But is he my dad?

'I'd forgotten it was there,' Mum whispers, more to herself than to me. 'I should have destroyed everything.'

'No!' I can't help shouting. I *want* to shout; I need my voice to be heard as I try to struggle through the layers of lies. 'Tell me the truth! The *truth*, Mum! I want to know why you've got two names, and why I have two dads and why you told me you had no family—'

'Anni,' Ace says softly, 'sit down and give your mum a chance to explain.'

Exhausted and afraid, I do as Ace says and collapse onto the sofa. But when Mum reaches out a hand to me, I ignore her and move further away.

'I don't know where to start,' Mum murmurs. There are tears in her eyes, but I don't care. My own harshness scares me a little, but I'm in self-preservation mode now. *Just tell me.*

'Start at the beginning,' Ace encourages her. God, I'm so glad she's here. 'Where were you born, Jamila?'

Mum's eyes are fixed on me, but Ace taps her hand gently to get her attention. 'Where were you born, Jamila?' she repeats.

Slowly Mum turns towards Ace. 'In London,' Mum replies automatically, robot-like. 'Chelsea.'

'You were brought up there?' Ace prompts her.

Mum nods. 'My parents owned a chain of very successful restaurants, and they made a lot of money. They wanted nothing but the very best for me and my three older brothers—'

She breaks off because I gasp aloud with shock, even though I'd already guessed this. 'You said you were an only child!' I shout, almost bursting with misery.

Mum hangs her head. 'I know. I'm sorry, darling.'

'Are your brothers alive or dead?' I demand. 'What about my grandparents?'

'I don't know.' The pain in Mum's voice twists my heart, but I won't let it stop me. Like Ace and the others, I'm now on a mission. 'I haven't seen any of them for years.'

'Why?' The knowledge that I might have relatives, a proper family whom I've never met, is impossible to take in. I might have living grandparents, uncles, aunts. Cousins too, if my mum's brothers have any children. This instant leap from loneliness is too overwhelming.

'Anni, let your mum tell her story,' Ace intervenes again, and I guess she already knows something of what Mum's going to say. Of course she does, she's read some of those newspaper articles hidden away in the box. 'You'll get answers to all your questions, and then you'll be able to understand everything.'

Understand? Never.

'We were a typical Asian family in that my mum and dad wanted us all to have brilliant careers,' Mum continues in a low voice. 'Two of my brothers went to Cambridge and one to Oxford. So everyone was thrilled when I won a place to study at Cambridge too. I wanted to become a lawyer and earn lots of money and make my parents proud; that's what I was focused on.' She pauses and, if possible, her face becomes even paler. The tears start to fall. 'At university I met Kanvar.'

'The guy in the picture?' Ace prompts her, for my benefit, I think. *Lawyers Kanvar and Jasmine Kapoor, founders of the environmental group RAIDERS, with their baby daughter, Anjeela.*

Mum nods. 'I was a good little student, but Kanvar was different. He came from the same kind of traditional Indian background as me, but he rebelled against his family, who were very wealthy – million-aires – and all they stood for. Kanvar was obsessed with the green and environmental issues that people had started to worry about in the 1990s; it was all he talked about. He was studying law too, not because he wanted to be rich, but because he wanted to make a difference.' Mum is crying continuously now and it's hard to make out what she's saying.

'Is he my dad?' I ask. Emotion swells inside me, so forceful I don't think my body can physically contain it. 'Is he my real dad?'

'Yes . . .' Mum breaks down now and Ace sits on the sofa and slips an arm around her shoulders. I cover my hands with my face. I don't know what to say; I don't know how to deal with this. How does anyone deal with something so earth-shattering? Now I under-stand why Mum hated talking about the past. Everything she had told me was untrue. *Everything*. It was all lies. Terrible, heart-breaking lies that are ripping me apart now.

My life as I thought it was is crumbling away into dust. The father I hardly knew, my dad Rajveer Rai, wasn't my father at all. He replaced another father whom I don't know either. I had two fathers, but in reality, I have none. *None*.

'Where's my dad now?' I demand. 'Why isn't he here? *Where's my real dad?*'

Mum sits staring into space, tears still falling down her cheeks. I don't know if she's even heard what I said. She seems to have returned to the past, to a place where I can't follow, and she's locked herself away there.

Ace gazes at me intently. 'Anni, I know this is hard,' she murmurs. 'But you'll find out the truth, I promise. Jamila, look at me.' Ace speaks softly, but there's a note of authority in her voice that Mum seems to respond to. She takes Mum's hands in her own and Mum turns to her obediently, like a child. 'What happened after you and Kanvar left university?'

'We got married straight away,' Mum replies, steadying herself although her eyes still hold that faraway look. 'We both got first-class degrees, so we found it pretty easy to complete our training and get jobs in a top legal firm in London.' Mum is clinging to Ace's hands as if that's the only thing giving her the strength to keep going. 'Then Kanvar's grandfather died and he received a very large inheritance. Millions and millions of pounds.'

Millions? I'm hanging onto Mum's every word. This is like a fairy story. But there won't be a happy-ever-after ending. I can see that in Ace's eyes.

'The two of you set up RAIDERS in the late 1990s, didn't you?' Ace prompts her.

'Yes, using Kanvar's inheritance.' Mum begins to speak more quickly, words spilling out as if they've been stored up inside her, waiting for an opportunity to be spoken all these years past. 'We bought a beautiful house in London with some of the money, but most of it went on starting up the group. It took off much faster than we ever imagined. Within a very short space of time we had hundreds of members. And thousands of pounds' worth of donations poured in every month. Kanvar and I left our jobs to run the group full-time.' The sadness in Mum's face is almost unbearable. 'Both our families were horrified and wanted nothing more to do with us.'

'You and Kanvar did a great job getting your message out there,' Ace says. 'I know one of the reasons you were so successful was because you took all that new technology like the internet, email and mobile phones, and used it to spread the word and organize protests.'

'That was Kanvar.' Mum smiles a little for the first time, remembering.

Kanvar. My dad. Where is he? I can't stand this any longer. I have to know.

Ace senses my frustration and shoots me a warning glance as Mum adds, 'He was so into all of that stuff. At first it was a hobby, but then it became serious.'

'The group hacked into the websites of oil companies and other big businesses, didn't they?' Ace asks. 'Trying to prove that there was a lot of illegal pollution and dumping of waste going on all around the world?'

Mum looks uneasy. 'Kanvar said it was justified because of what they were doing,' she murmurs. 'They were ruining the planet for us, our children and our grandchildren. After Anni was born, all these issues seemed even more important now we had our own child. But as a result of what we were doing, the group made some serious enemies. We started to receive anonymous threats almost every single day.' Mum's voice begins to falter, and I can see the tears coming once more. 'Then, when we bought the *Rebel*

Raider . . .' She sinks her head into her hands and can't say any more because she's crying too hopelessly.

'The *Rebel Raider*?' I repeat, frustrated.

Ace has taken out her iPhone. She gazes at me and I can see compassion and understanding in her face. She knows all this already. 'I just read about it in those newspaper articles, Anni. The group bought a ship, an old fishing trawler, so that they could protest about whale-hunting and attempt to stop it. About eleven years ago a large number of them sailed to Scandinavia to try and disrupt the whale-hunting season—' Ace breaks off. 'Jamila, do you want to tell Anni what happened?' But Mum is lost in her memories and in her tears.

'You tell me, Ace,' I say hoarsely. 'I just want to know.'

With a few brief taps, Ace pulls up a news website on her phone. Then, silently, she hands it to me.

The newspaper headline reads:

FOUR KILLED AS PROTEST SHIP THE *REBEL RAIDER* RUNS AGROUND IN SCANDINAVIAN WATERS. And, underneath: RAIDERS FOUNDER KANVAR KAPOOR DROWNS, WIFE JASMINE IS INJURED.

The black words swim together into a blur, but certain phrases and sentences jump out at me. '*RAIDERS co-founder Jasmine Kapoor sustained serious leg injuries ... Ship was sabotaged ... Whale-hunters deny responsibility ... Kanvar Kapoor drowns ...*'

I return Ace's phone to her and sit in stupefied silence. I don't know what to focus on first. That my dad isn't who I thought he was. That he died fighting for a cause he passionately believed in. That my mum – *my mum* – was a lawyer and a committed green activist who boldly took risks and occasionally broke the law. That I'm not on my own and might actually have relatives – real, living people who are my own flesh and blood. I look back down the years and all I can see is a thick veil of lies, blotting out the truth of who I really am.

'Jamila, did you disband the group after Kanvar died?' Ace asks quietly as, finally, Mum's sobs begin to slow down.

'I had no choice.' Mum is lost in the past again, and her voice trembles with emotion. 'Everything was finished. The group was still being threatened. Kanvar's family blamed me for what had happened to him, and they wanted custody of Anni. So did my own parents. They'd looked after Anni while I was in hospital, and thought she ought to live with them. They were trying to be kind, but I couldn't give Anni up, she was all I had left . . . And I was still getting anonymous threats . . . They'd already got Kanvar, and they knew all about my family, and about Anni . . .' Mum glances at me. I stare back at her, stony-faced, trying to conceal how much her words are affecting me. 'I decided I had to disappear. Once I was well enough, I changed my name, sold our house and moved miles away. Rajveer helped me to start a new life.'

The man I had thought was my dad.

'Rajveer was someone you knew already?' says Ace. She's filling in the gaps for me – I know it and I'm grateful, but it's all too much. I can hardly take in what I've already heard.

'He was one of RAIDERS' biggest supporters,' Mum replies. 'If it wasn't for him, I don't know what I would have done . . .'

Mum talks on, more freely, still tearful occasionally,

but becoming calmer, as if it's a relief to tell her story at last. Every time she went out, she was afraid, Mum says, that someone was following her, watching her, someone who wanted to hurt us or maybe someone from my dad's family or even her own looking to snatch me away from her. Mum says my stepfather loved me like I was his own daughter. Just a couple of years later, though, he died too, leaving Mum the house and everything he owned. But there was hardly any money left as by then he'd been ill with leukaemia for months, and his antiques business was almost bankrupt.

Mum couldn't bring herself to leave the house, though. It was the one and only place she felt safe. And so the agoraphobia tightened its sinister grip on her until she couldn't go outside at all. Mum tells Ace that, since then, she and I have been living on the money from the sale of our old family home in London.

Mum is saying all this, and I can hear her, but my head is pounding and bursting and it feels too full of words. I thought my world had shattered yesterday, when Ace and the others showed up. Was it really only last night? But that was nothing compared to how I feel right now. My one constant, my relationship with my mum, the one thing I really believed in, has been torn apart and now lies trampled in the dust. I'm blazing with anger and hurt.

I jump to my feet, grab the keys Ace has left on the table and run from the room.

'Anni!' Mum calls.

I don't stop. I hear a thud behind me, and then Ace curses loudly and I realize she's probably leaped up to follow me and tripped over one of Mum's sticks lying on the floor. Good. It gives me the few seconds' advantage that I need.

I turn the key, slip the bolts and fling the front door open.

The cold, fresh air hits me in the face and wraps itself around me.

Then I run away.

Saturday 8 November, 6.21 a.m.

It's still dark outside, but I'm out of the front garden in under a minute, climbing over the locked iron gate, and I take off down the road. Freedom should feel exhilarating and wonderful, but it doesn't. I'm trapped in a different prison now, one inside my own head.

I run faster. I don't know why I have to keep going, but it's almost as if I'm trying to escape from everything I've just been told. Instinctively I avoid the area where police officers will surely be waiting, ready for the Prime Minister's arrival later today. Any police officer would be well suspicious if he or she saw a twelve-year-old girl running for her life this early in the morning. But I can't stop, not yet. I don't know where I'm running to, and I don't care.

I know I should find a police officer and tell him or her about Ace and the others, but I can't. What's just happened to me is so huge, it's impossible to concentrate on anything else.

My dad, Kanvar Kapoor, is dead.

Rajveer Rai was my stepfather, not my real dad.

Mum lied to me all along.

I might have family, somewhere . . .

These words pound through my mind in time with the rhythm of my running feet. They replay over and over and over again until, eventually, I can't physically go any further, and I begin to slow down. My lungs are gasping for air, my heart's thudding mercilessly against my chest and my muscles are burning. For the first time I come to a halt and look around to see where I am. I'm outside the same park I cut through on the way home from school, although I've arrived by a different, longer, route. After what has happened since I was here yesterday, I'm now a completely different person, but I'm not convinced this is a good thing. My thoughts whirl between the past, the present and my future. At this moment, all three of them seem shockingly unstable.

A familiar voice behind me. 'You're a fast runner.'

It's Ace. She's taken off her balaclava again and she's panting, pressing one hand to her side. 'I nearly lost you a few times,' she adds, taking out her phone.

I can hardly believe it's her. 'What are you doing here?'

'Your mum asked me to follow you,' Ace says as she fires off a quick text. 'She was frantic when you ran out of the house. I'm just letting Jack know you're safe so he can tell her.'

'What does *she* care?' I retort bitterly. 'She lied to me! All these years, she lied to me!'

'I know.' Ace takes my arm and guides me to a bench just outside the park gates, where she sits me down. 'This must be hell for you, Anni. I understand that. It'd be hugely difficult, almost impossible, for anyone to cope with what you've just found out.' She slips her arm around my shoulders. 'Listen to me, Anni. I know you're going to get through this—'

'You *don't* know!' I yell, pulling away from her. 'That's just words, just stuff people say!'

Ace shakes her head. 'No, it isn't. It's true. I can say that and mean it because, from the moment I met you, you've shown me exactly what kind of person you are.'

'What do you mean?'

'You're a fighter, Anni,' Ace replies in a brisk, no-nonsense voice. 'A real, honest-to-goodness fighter through and through. You hardly ever give up and give in. You've got brains, you've got strength and you've got a big heart. You're one in a million, believe me.'

I can tell she does mean it. I start crying hopelessly and I can't answer her.

'And you know where all those qualities come from?' Ace goes on. 'From your mum and dad. Why do you think RAIDERS became so successful so quickly? Why were some big companies so afraid of them? Because your parents are amazing people, that's why. And you're just like them.'

'I'm not, I'm not,' I gulp between sobs. 'I didn't even know my real dad, and now I never will.'

'But your mum can tell you all about him,' Ace says gently. 'She can make him come alive for you. And you'll find out new things about your mum too. She was just as involved with the group as your dad.

She had a whole different life before her accident, a life you know nothing about.'

'I just wish she hadn't lied to me. I *trusted* her, Ace!'

'I know it's impossibly difficult, but try to see things from your mum's point of view, Anni.' Ace speaks firmly, seriously. 'She lost her husband in a terrible accident. She had hardly anyone to turn to because her family and your dad's were angry with her, and they wanted custody of you. RAIDERS, the group she and your dad believed in so passionately, was falling apart. Not only that, she was recovering from her own horrific injuries, but above all, she was desperate to protect you. What your mum did to try and make a new life for herself and for you – especially after your stepfather died too and she was alone – took an enormous amount of courage.'

I can see this. I really can. But my wounds are so deep and so painful I don't know if they will ever heal.

'Why didn't she just tell me the truth when I got older?' I demand, but I know I'm asking the wrong person. Only Mum herself can explain that.

'I can't know for sure, but I'm guessing your mum

just wanted to forget all about what had happened. Maybe she thought it was better for both of you to leave the past behind. Safer.'

We sit there in silence for a few moments.

'I told you how I remembered hearing bits and pieces about RAIDERS on the TV news when I was very young,' Ace tells me. 'I didn't know much about green issues or politics then, but I loved the energy they had and all the crazy publicity stunts they pulled. It was one of the reasons I joined—' She bites her lip, just managing, I guess, to stop herself from revealing the name of the protest group to which she and the others belong. 'Anyway, your parents and others like them inspired me to care, Anni. To want to make a difference. I really and truly admire them both.'

I glance at Ace and can see nothing but honesty in her face.

'You've been surrounded by people who love you, Anni,' Ace reminds me. 'Your dad, your mum, even your stepdad, who cared for you like his own daughter. You might have other family out there whom you can finally get to know. Then you won't be so alone and isolated any more. You'll talk to your mum and you'll get through this and I know you'll be all right. I trust you to be OK, because I know what kind of girl you are.'

'I hope you're right.' My voice wobbles. 'I don't want to hate my mum. I do love her, but—'

'Try to remember why she did what she did,' Ace suggests. 'Did your mum do it to hurt you or to protect you? There's the difference.'

And of course, I know why Mum did it. Anger still burns inside me, but the fire has cooled slightly, and suddenly I'm filled with the most desperate longing to return to Mum and hear what she's got to say, to ask all the questions I need to ask and then to deal with the answers in my own way.

'Ready to go home?' asks Ace.

'Ready.' I stand up.

But there's a long, hard road ahead and this is only the first step.

Saturday 8 November, 6.45 a.m.

Morning is dawning and the sun is rising, chasing away the darkness.

Ace and I walk back to the house in a companionable silence that would have been unthinkable yesterday. We return by a different, shorter route, although not the shortest as that would have taken us right down the road the Prime Minister will travel very soon. Nevertheless, as we pause at a pedestrian crossing, a police car on patrol crawls past us. The policewoman in the passenger seat gives us a keen glance and my heart lurches. But the car moves on and doesn't stop.

'We won't go to the police,' I say quietly. 'After you've gone, I mean.'

'Your mum might feel differently,' Ace replies. 'She'll do what she thinks is right.'

'You've helped us.' The words come out

awkwardly, but Ace can't miss the real gratitude in my voice. 'If it wasn't for you, I'd never have found out – all this. Everything would still be the same, but now . . . Well, things have to be different, don't they?'

'I hope so,' Ace replies as we turn into our street.

'What's your real name?' I blurt out. 'Sorry, you don't have to tell me if you don't want to.'

Ace hesitates for a moment, then shrugs. 'Sarika,' she replies. It suits her.

We reach the garden gate. Then I see the most amazing thing. A truly unbelievable, wonderful sight.

The front door is open. My mum is outside – *outside!* – standing in the porch, supporting herself on her sticks. Her face is terrified yet determined. Behind her I can see King, Jack and Queenie hovering anxiously, ready to catch her if she falls.

This is the furthest my mum has been out of the house for years.

I understand how much courage, willpower and effort it's taken her just to get this far. I also know she's done this for me, and me only. It is then I realize that love is a million times more powerful than hate.

So, despite everything, I break away from Ace and I run through the garden and Mum drops her sticks and we hug each other almost to death. The time for words is later.

Saturday 8 November, 10.00 a.m.

For the next few hours, despite having been awake almost all night, Mum and I talk until we've exhausted everything we want to say. For the moment. Ace and the others are busy in the attic as they put the final touches to their preparations, but Mum and I hardly think about what they're doing or even remember that they're there. The mystery that's consumed me all night is taking second place to the story of my own life, a story more fascinating and frustrating than anything I've ever read.

Mum answers my questions honestly and I shout and scream and we argue and we cry, but in the end, we both know we'll manage to work this out because we love each other. There'll be more heart-to-heart talks and more question-and-answer sessions and probably more arguments, and I know that when the time is right, I'll reveal my own secret to Mum. But, as Ace said, we'll come through it all, somehow.

'Anni, I want things to be different from now on,' Mum tells me earnestly. 'This is no life for you. I've been feeling guilty for years. I want to get help. You deserve better than this.'

'So do you, Mum,' I tell her. 'We'll do this together.'

The prospect of a new, exciting life is opening up before me like a flower bud unfurling, and I have to keep reminding myself this is all really happening as Mum talks about seeing doctors and being treated for her illnesses and – amazingly – even the possibility of selling this house. Maybe even contacting her family again, as well as my dad's. As Mum says, they might have been searching for us all these years without us knowing it. My dreary, grey life is suddenly being repainted in the bright, shining colours of light and hope.

Mum and I sit, deep in discussion, making plans. We're so involved with each other it's a shock when Ace comes in a few hours later.

'It's almost ten,' she says. 'We hope you'll join us in the attic.'

'You mean – we're going to see what you've been doing all night?' I ask a little uncertainly.

Ace nods. 'If you want to, that is. You might prefer not to know.'

'No way!' My curiosity instantly fires up again. This is the final piece of the mystery, the explanation for everything that's happened. 'I definitely want to see.'

'So do I,' Mum agrees.

Ace and I help Mum onto her sticks and we go out into the hall. Jack and Queenie are waiting for us at the top of the main staircase. When we reach the attics, King is outside on the landing. They've all taken off their balaclavas.

'Ready?' Ace asks him.

King nods. 'We'd better get on with it. We only have a couple of minutes.'

He reaches for the door handle. For a moment I feel ablaze with uncertainty and my heart begins to thud unpleasantly because I have no idea what I'm going to find when I step inside the attic.

King opens the door slowly, carefully, as if he's

worried he might hit something on the other side. I strain forward to get that first glimpse into the room.

The very first thing I notice is a round black bomb lying directly in front of me on the attic floor. Even as I gasp with alarm and instinctively move to protect Mum, I'm already realizing that what I *think* I'm seeing isn't what it really is. The 'bomb' is, in fact, a black balloon shaped to look like a bomb, a 'fuse' of white string trailing from the top. Attached at the other end of the string is a star-shaped piece of yellow cellophane, as if someone's just lit the fuse with a match. It's the kind of funny, old-fashioned bomb you see in cartoons that explodes when someone picks it up and sets their hair and eyebrows on fire.

The attic is filled with these black bombs, alongside big, regular-shaped white balloons. All the balloons bob gently up and down on the floor like a striking black-and-white carpet. There are piles of them, floating around and jostling each other for space. I can't guess how many, but maybe hundreds.

'This is what you've been doing?' I ask faintly. 'Blowing up balloons? All this time?'

'We did have some help,' Queenie admits. 'We brought some balloon pumps with us.'

And then I see that there is printed writing, red letters, on the white balloons. Each one carries a short slogan:

People Power!

Don't Sell Out to the Banks.

People, not Profits.

Children are The Future – End Child Poverty.

If You Think Education is Expensive, Try Ignorance.

Help The Lost Generation – More Jobs For Young People.

Support the NHS.

And there are others about university fees, big companies not paying their taxes and public spending cuts.

'Like I told you from the start, Anni, we're not going to hurt anyone,' Ace reminds me. 'This is a peaceful protest. That's how our group works. For now.'

'But when we release the balloons, we'll be

disrupting the Prime Minister's visit,' Jack explains, 'so we have to be careful or they'll stop us – they'll think of some reason why it would be illegal or something – and it wouldn't get on the telly. Which is what we want to happen.'

'We couldn't allow ourselves to get caught, not on our very first mission.' Ace speaks quietly. 'Because this is only the beginning.'

'What do you mean?' I pounce on her words, but Ace simply shakes her head.

'Let's get on with it,' King says impatiently. 'His car'll be passing by any minute.'

Ace, King, Queenie and Jack wade through a sea of bouncing, bobbing black and white towards the three big windows. They pull back the thick curtains, and winter sunlight pours into the attic. As they fling the windows open one by one, things click into place inside my head, and I finally see the whole picture. The silver object I thought was a gun – probably part of a balloon pump. That *bang* I heard from behind the closed door – almost certainly a balloon bursting. Now everything makes sense.

A light breeze rushes into the attic, stirring the balloons and tossing them around. Mum and I watch as the four protestors begin scooping the balloons up, throwing them out of the windows, armfuls at a time. The black and white balloons sail away on the wind, taking the slogans with them for all to see.

'The wind's in just about the right direction,' Jack pants, chucking another load of black bombs out into the sky. 'Some of them will probably float right over the PM's car. How lucky is that?'

'Hope the press get some fabulous photos when he arrives at the hospital,' Queenie laughs. 'Think of all that great publicity we're going to get, folks!'

'And the PM will be squirming with embarrassment,' King adds gleefully. 'Result!'

'Hurry,' Ace urges them. 'We need to get all these balloons out before anyone realizes where they're coming from.'

They're pushing the last lot of balloons out now, and I run over to one of the windows to help.

'This is for you, Dad,' I whisper, throwing an armful of balloons out into the sky. When I say the word

'Dad', there are two faces inside my head, and both of them are a part of me.

Mum joins me and manages to knock a couple of white balloons out into the sky with one of her sticks. The big houses in front of us block our view some-what and so I can only catch glimpses of the Prime Minister's big black car and his police escort. But I can see that most of the balloons are heading in the direc-tion of the hospital. In the streets nearest us, I look down on people looking up. At first, some seem alarmed, pointing at the black balloons and then duck-ing for cover. But, like me, they realize almost instantly that the 'bombs' aren't real. They stand staring up at the sky as it rains black and white, and little children run around, trying to catch the balloons.

'How did you know exactly when the Prime Minister was arriving at the hospital?' I ask curiously.

Queenie taps the side of her nose and winks at me. 'Insider information,' she confides. 'Someone who works at the hospital tipped us off.' Then she whoops with delight as, in the distance, we see one of the 'bombs' bounce onto the roof of the Prime Minister's car and then burst as it's punctured by the aerial. 'Think we scored a direct hit there, guys!'

'Quick, close the windows,' Ace orders as the last balloon floats outside. King, Queenie and Jack jump forward to do so, and then I can almost see the tension drain out of their bodies. All four break into cheers and high-fives and hugs.

Then Ace turns to Mum and me. 'That's it,' she says softly. 'We're done.'

Mum nods, almost as if she approves. 'I'm impressed you used latex balloons to make your protest, and didn't use helium,' she says unexpectedly. 'Latex is a little less environmentally toxic because it's supposed to decompose more quickly.'

Ace nods. 'We try to be as green as possible with our protests. And we have some of our members on the ground, ready to collect up as much of the debris as they can. Though we hope people generally will take most of the balloons home and think about what's written on them.' She and Mum smile at each other, and I see a shared understanding between them.

'Ace.' King is standing by the attic door, ready to make a quick getaway. He sounds nervous. 'We ought to leave. Right away, before the police come knocking.'

'Yes.' Ace looks at Mum again. 'The police will probably want to question everyone around this area to find out who's to blame, if they haven't worked out where the balloons are coming from already.'

Mum shrugs. 'Everyone has the right to peaceful protest,' she says quietly. 'I've stood up to the police more than a few times myself in the past. And sometimes – well, Kanvar and I did things that weren't strictly legal because we were looking at the bigger picture. We won't be telling anyone anything, will we, Anni?'

Relieved, I shake my head.

'Ace, come *on*.' Jack has joined King by the door, and Queenie is hovering there too. 'We need to go.'

I'm quiet, not speaking because I'm feeling hopelessly confused right now. Ace and the others are going; at last, the one thing I've been hoping and praying for is finally happening. And yet . . . From a frightening presence, from being intruders in our house, they've become almost like . . . friends. I know how ridiculous this sounds. But I don't want them to leave.

And still Ace hesitates. 'Can I come and see you again?' she blurts out unexpectedly. I've never heard Ace the leader, Ace the control freak, sound so uncertain and unsure of herself. 'It'd be awesome to hear more about RAIDERS, if you didn't mind talking about it. And to see how you're both getting on, of course.'

I glance at Mum. 'Yes, say yes,' I whisper. And as I do so, I realize that things have definitely changed because now Mum is very definitely the adult and I'm the child. I'm not responsible for everything any more, and it feels good.

'Of course,' Mum replies in a strong, confident voice. 'But don't leave it too long, Ace, because we'll be moving from this house sometime very soon.'

Ace smiles. Her eyes meet mine briefly, and then she strides across the attic to join the others. Jack grins at me while Queenie and King raise their hands in farewell. They disappear down the stairs and they're gone. Just like that. We don't even hear them collect their stuff and leave the house.

Silently Mum and I turn back to the window. I slip my arm around Mum's waist. We stand and watch the balloons floating across the sky, and we look forward to our new life and our freedom, at last.

Agoraphobia

Agoraphobia is a fear of being in situations where escape might be difficult, or help wouldn't be available if things go wrong. For instance, a person suffering from agoraphobia may be scared of leaving home, travelling on public transport or visiting a crowded public place. If people with agoraphobia find themselves in a stressful situation they usually experience symptoms of a panic attack, such as rapid breathing, feeling hot and sweaty, and feeling sick.

Like Anni's mum, they avoid situations that cause anxiety and may only leave the house with a friend or relative, or order groceries online rather than go to the supermarket.

There are lots of treatments available to help people who suffer from agoraphobia. If you – or someone you care about – are affected by this condition, get in touch with your doctor first.

You can also find out some helpful information about agoraphobia here:

www.nhs.uk/conditions/agoraphobia

www.anxietycare.org.uk/docs/agoraphobia.asp

www.time-to-change.org.uk/category/blog/phobias

Young Carers

Although Anni doesn't realize it, she is what is known as a 'young carer' – someone aged eighteen or under who helps look after a relative who has a condition such as a disability, illness, mental health condition, or a drug or alcohol problem. The majority of young carers do jobs in and around the home, such as cooking, cleaning, or helping someone to get dressed and move around. Young carers may need to help a relative deal with their feelings by talking to them, listening and trying to understand their problems.

The difference between young carers and other young people who help in the home is that young carers are often responsible for someone else in their family in a way that most other young people aren't.

If you think you might be a young carer, there are lots of places where you can find support and further information. You may even be eligible for a Carer's Allowance.

Friends and family

Talking to a friend or a relative about any problems can be helpful. People who find it hard to talk to others often write down their thoughts in a diary, poem or letter first. You can also chat with one another on the Young Carers' Net website (www.youngcarers.net/) and get lots of advice and support from other young people.

Teachers and other school staff

Teachers are there to help pupils get the most out of school. They can be a good person for you to speak to about any problems you have. If you're getting angry in school, missing lessons to help look after someone at home, or struggling to get your work in on time, you might benefit from talking to a teacher.

Social workers

A social worker's job is to support and help a family

that might be having difficulties. A social worker only finds a new home for a child if the child is in danger at home and there's no other way of keeping them safe. Social workers may be asked to help a young carer's family if there are problems that the family members are struggling to sort out on their own.

If you feel you need help staying healthy and taking part in school and social activities, you might be able to get help. In some cases, support workers can help you with your education and health.

Healthcare professionals

If you have concerns about your own health, or the health of the person you care for, you can speak to a doctor or GP in a safe and confidential environment.

School nurses visit schools and are normally happy to speak to young people about any other concerns they might have.

Counsellors work in a variety of places, including schools, hospitals and youth centres. A counsellor's job is to listen carefully and give advice in a private setting.

You may find it useful to talk to someone con-
fidentially. Helplines are a good way of doing this.
In the UK, you can call Carers Direct on 0300 123
1053 for confidential information and advice.
ChildLine also has a confidential listening service for
children and young people. Call 0800 1111.

You can also find out some helpful information
here:

www.youngcarers.net/

www.nhs.uk/carersdirect/young/